THE NURSERY RHYME MURDERS

Mr. Budd and Sergeant Leek investigate a peculiar murder in the village of Marbury. A body has been found in a derelict house called 'Jackson's Folly'. A note, pinned to the door, has the nursery rhyme 'The House That Jack Built' scribbled on it. Then Lady Conyers of nearby Marbury Court is also found dead in bed — with the same rhyme scrawled on the bedroom door ... As Mr. Budd encounters many false trails, can he secure a successful conclusion?

GERALD VERNER

◆

THE NURSERY RHYME MURDERS

Complete and Unabridged

LINFORD
Leicester

First published in Great Britain

First Linford Edition
published 2011

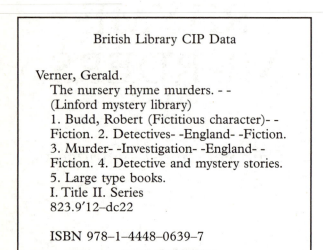

British Library CIP Data

Verner, Gerald.
  The nursery rhyme murders. - -
(Linford mystery library)
1. Budd, Robert (Fictitious character)- -
Fiction. 2. Detectives- -England- -Fiction.
3. Murder- -Investigation- -England- -
Fiction. 4. Detective and mystery stories.
5. Large type books.
I. Title II. Series
823.9'12–dc22

ISBN 978–1–4448–0639–7

Published by
F. A. Thorpe (Publishing)
Anstey, Leicestershire

Set by Words & Graphics Ltd.
Anstey, Leicestershire
Printed and bound in Great Britain by
T. J. International Ltd., Padstow, Cornwall

This book is printed on acid-free paper

1

When Mr. Sam Sprigot, known to the police as 'Stackpipe Sam', because of his partiality for entering other peoples houses by this method, came out of prison after serving a three-year sentence, his first act was to make a telephone call. After that his movements became obscure. He turned up in London three months later, found a quiet room in a dingy back street near the Waterloo Road, where for several weeks he lay upon his bed, smoking and reading the newspapers and only venturing out into the streets after darkness had fallen, when he would go for long nocturnal rambles, never taking the same route twice, and always returning to his lodgings before the first streaks of dawn appeared over the house-tops.

His landlady, after the manner of her kind, at first displayed some curiosity regarding these midnight excursions, but after he had explained that he worked as a night watchman at a large factory nearby, she quickly lost interest in him and returned to the more fruitful occupation of watching the behaviour of her nearest neighbours which had been for many years an absorbing passion.

Quiet and inoffensive, a rather pathetic-looking little man with watery eyes and a long thin nose, Sam was hardly the type to attract attention, and within a few weeks he became so much a part of his drab background as to be almost unnoticable. He had no visitors, received no letters, and apart from an occasional 'Good-morning' or a few words with his landlady when he settled his bill, he was never seen to hold any communication with anyone. It was, therefore, with no little surprise that his landlady found an envelope in the letter-box one morning addressed to her unassuming lodger.

She held it up to the light, hoping to be able to decipher some of the contents, for Mrs. Bagley's bump of curiosity was very highly developed, but the paper was too thick and defied all her effort. She was just considering taking it to the kitchen and steaming the envelope open when the sound of her lodger's door, opening above, startled her. Looking up she saw Mr. Sprigot staring down at her.

'Is that for me?' he inquired.

For a moment she felt an impulse to retain the letter until she had had a chance to find out what was in it, and say it had come by a later post. But he had already seen the envelope and would, as likely as not, recognise it again.

She held it out to him a little reluctantly.

She saw his face change as he saw the writing on the envelope. Never a very good colour it turned to a sickly greenish hue. His small, moist eyes widened and he put out a shaking hand to steady himself by the banisters. Suddenly pulling himself together, he mumbled an incoherent word of thanks, stumbled up the stairs to his room, and slammed the door.

Mrs. Bagley stared after him, her curiosity at fever heat. Why had the letter had such an extraordinary effect on her lodger? She went into her kitchen and poured herself out a cup of strong tea. He had obviously been expecting it and yet the sight of it had reduced him to a state bordering on collapse.

Mrs. Bagley licked her lips. Here was something that was really interesting. She pondered deeply as she drank her oversweetened tea. The behaviour of her neighbours had been very monotonous lately. Life was very dull for Mrs. Bagley. A really good piece of scandal, now . . . She sighed and shrugged her shoulders as she poured herself out a second cup of tea. Why hadn't she kept the letter back and found out its contents? Ah well, it was too late now. Perhaps there was really nothing in it after all . . .

There she was wrong.

During the brief moment the letter had been in her possession, she had held in her hand the clue to a mystery that was to puzzle some of the best brains in the country. Deep down below the surface, something evil was stirring from a long slumber and with its waking bringing a trail of terror and sudden death.

All that day it had rained steadily, but towards nightfall it stopped, and when Sam Sprigot slipped quietly out of Mrs. Bagley's front door and closed it gently behind him, a light breeze had sprung up.

It was very dark. The moon would not be up for another hour yet, and it was with a feeling of relief that Sam left the little back streets, with their dim gas lights, for the better lights and bustle of the main thoroughfares.

The cinemas had just broken and the streets were thronged with people returning to their homes after their evening's amusement. Nobody took much notice of the seedy little man who slunk along the pavement with his collar turned up and his soft hat pulled down over his eyes, and turned every now and again to look back over his shoulder as though he might be fearful of what he should see behind him.

After walking for some time he turned into a public house and ordered a double Johnny Walker. He gulped half of it, took out a packet of cigarettes, lit one, and inhaled deeply.

'Last orders, please,' called the barmaid. 'Time ter go 'ome ter bye-byes.'

Sam finished his drink and ordered another. It was just on half-past ten by the big clock behind the bar. He drank his second whisky, buttoned up his coat, and went out into the street. They were emptier now — most of the people had already gone home.

Sam boarded a bus for Victoria. From there he travelled by Underground to Earls Court and worked his way from there, by a circuitous route, to Waterloo. He just had time to catch the last train to Marbury. It was not very full and he found himself an empty compartment. Sinking back into a corner seat, he took out the letter he had received that morning and read it through several times. When the train had pulled out from the platform and was well on its way, he took out a box of matches from his pocket, set fire to the letter, and carefully stamped out the ashes.

It was nearly two o'clock when he

arrived at Marbury, a small way-side station that seemed to have little excuse for its existence and was really little more than a halt. He was the only passenger to alight, and after waiting a few minutes to make sure that he had not been followed, he gave up his ticket to the sleepy-eyed porter and set off down the long, deserted country road that led from the station to the village.

Presently he came to a fork in the road. He hesitated a moment before he turned into the right hand road and continued on until he came to the entrance to a narrow lane which sloped away steeply into the darkness. Somewhere behind the heavy clouds there was a moon, but it was very dark and the rain had started again — a thin, wetting drizzle. Sam shivered and pulled his coat closer round his lean body. He could hear in the distance a dog howling mournfully as he stumbled cautiously over the uneven surface of the lane. He swore softly to himself as dripping leaves brushed his face and his feet slithered in the deep ruts and cart-tracks. After a little while the ground began to rise again and he found the going easier. It was lighter now, the trees were thinning, and presently he found himself in the open. On either side the country stretched away to woods and hills but a little way in front of him, backed by a patch of trees, loomed the massive bulk of a house.

Mr. Sprigot stopped, breathing a little heavily, and surveyed it without enthusiasm.

'So that's the perishin' place, is it?' he muttered under his breath.

The house was obviously a ruin. The gate leading up the short drive was broken and hanging drunkenly from its hinges. The weeds grew thickly. The overhanging roof of the porch had fallen and lay across the steps leading up to the front door.

Sam approached stealthily. His heart was thumping in his thin chest and he would have given a lot for the lights of the streets he had left behind him earlier. The ground floor windows were all broken and the tattered remnants of torn blinds flapped behind them in the wind. For a moment he felt a sudden strong desire to go back — to leave this decaying and derelict house and run as fast as he could until it was far behind him. But he fought down this urge and walked slowly up to the gaping cavity where the front door had once been. It was still there, he saw, as he drew nearer, but smashed and broken like everything else about the place.

Far away in the distance the dog howled again, and Sam Sprigot felt the hair on his neck stir unpleasantly. But he summoned up his rapidly waning courage and crept in through the broken door into the dark cavern of the hall. There was a squeaking and scampering of rats and a smell of mildew and decay. With hands outspread before him he edged his way into the darkness. His foot struck against a hard obstacle and at the same moment his groping fingers came in contact with something soft and silky. He stepped quickly backwards and fumbling with shaking hands found his matches and struck one.

He was standing in what remained of

the hall. On one side, amid the rotting, broken panelling, jutted out a huge stone fireplace. On the other a short flight of stairs led down through an archway to the back portion of the house. In front of him rose the main staircase, dividing half-way to join a gallery which ran round the entire upper part of the huge hall.

And on the lower newel-post of this staircase was the thing his fingers had touched. It gleamed in the light of the match with rainbow colours.

A woman's scarf!

The match burned his fingers and went out. As the darkness closed in on him he heard a sound behind him and swung round.

From somewhere in the darkness of that ruined hall somebody chuckled softly . . .

2

The Reverend Oswald Hornbeam yawned, stretched, and finally awoke with a feeling of deep contentment. The morning was bright and clear. The sun was filtering through the drawn blinds and outside a blackbird carolled happily.

Mr. Hornbeam consulted the small clock on his bedside table. Half-past six. There was another hour yet before he need get up. He turned over on his side and prepared to doze off again. Downstairs he could hear the sound of old Sarah unbolting the back door. Soon she would be lighting the kitchen fire, and then the clatter of plates and dishes would announce the preparation of breakfast.

Breakfast!

It was the Reverend Oswald Hornbeam's favourite meal. However difficult the day before had been, or the day to come might be, Mr. Hornbeam always enjoyed his breakfast. He never allowed anything to interfere with that enjoyment. Battle, murder, and sudden death might come later but breakfast was a ritual that took precedence before everything.

And this morning there would be bacon — bacon and mushrooms!

Mr. Hornbeam wrinkled his large nose in joyous anticipation. And then he suddenly sat up in bed with a jerk. He had forgotten the mushrooms!

Last night he had tied a knot in his handkerchief to remind himself — and then he had gone to bed and forgotten all about it.

He glanced at the bedside clock again. There was still time if he hurried. He would go down to the meadow behind Jackson's Folly where there were usually a good crop. If only Mrs. Suggins's little boy hadn't been there before him . . . Perhaps, however, this morning he had overslept.

Muttering a fervent prayer that this might be so, Mr. Hornbeam hastily got out of bed and reached for his trousers . . .

Three-quarters of an hour later with a

basket filled with edible fungi, Mr. Hornbeam was returning happily to the rectory when he saw something which made him pause and frown. He had taken a short cut through the grounds of Jackson's Folly, the derelict house which was such an eye-sore to the villagers, and the shattered front door was open and swinging in the wind.

An expression of annoyance crossed Mr. Hornbeam's usually placid face. How many times had he impressed upon his parishoners, that although the house was empty it was not necessarily public property. He had mentioned it more than once from the pulpit and now . . . Somebody had been here. The door when he had last seen it had been wedged shut with a wooden bar. It was too bad! He would have to tell old Penworthy to fasten it up properly with a padlock. This was the third time in three weeks . . .

He put down his basket and went up to the door with the intention of doing what he could to shut it securely. As he came nearer, he saw that there was a sheet of paper pinned on the broken panel.

Curious, he thought, what could it be? Some nonsense of the local children probably. The younger generation were becoming very difficult these days. No respect for anything. Only last week, one of them had done a drawing of Miss Titmarsh — a really most libellous drawing — and pinned it on her gate. And she had insisted that it was the work of Major Panting. Ridiculous! As if the major would play silly tricks like that. Really, these women were most stupid — most stupid.

The Reverend Oswald sighed. Life was not always easy in a village. It was surprising how difficult people could be. Even quite nice people like Lady Conyers, had their awkward moments. Look how difficult she had been with the Gibson girl last week? Still she had a lot to put up with. That husband of hers gave her a lot of trouble — gambling all the money away on horses. Poor woman — it was a good thing she had money of her own. She had been a great help to the church.

Mr. Hornbeam had been fumbling for

his spectacles — without them he was as blind as a bat — now he put them on and peered at the paper pinned to the door.

It was as he had thought. The work of one of the children. He was glad to say that it was nothing of an unpleasant kind. One never knew *what* to expect these days. No, nothing unpleasant . . .

It was roughly printed in blue pencil on a page torn from an exercise book and appeared to be part of a nursery rhyme.

'THIS IS THE RAT THAT ATE THE MALT THAT LAY IN THE HOUSE THAT JACK BUILT.'

★ ★ ★

Quite appropriate, of course. The place was known in the district as Jackson's Folly. But what a strange thing to write. Still it might have been worse. Obviously it had been done by one of the nicer types of children. Probably he had learnt it at school. Vaguely, Mr. Hornbeam remembered hearing it recently when he had passed by the schoolhouse. Miss Titmarsh had been taking the infant class. She always insisted on teaching them the old nursery rhymes. Ah well, there was nothing like them.

Mr. Hornbeam looked absently into the dark hall before closing the front door and doing what he could to fasten it. There was a dim shaft of sunlight, falling from some hole or other, that threw a faint light on the foot of the big staircase. Just out of the light was what looked like a bundle of old clothes.

The Reverend Oswald went in and walked towards this bundle to see what it was. His large, placid face went white as he saw . . .

It was the body of a little, thin man that lay huddled up by the foot of the staircase, and the manner of his death was beyond dispute for his head had been crushed by a heavy blow and the blood surrounding it was still wet . . .

★ ★ ★

For more than three centuries the people of Marbury had looked up to the Conyers family, and the Conyers family, in more senses than one, had looked down upon the people of Marbury. Marbury Court, built by the first Sir William Conyers in 1672, a fine example of Restoration architecture and one of the show places of the neighbourhood, stood upon a slight hill, and from its wide stone terraces and finely proportioned windows the village could be seen spread out below it — a pleasantly peaceful picture of rural England at its best.

Clustered round the village green a score of timbered cottages dozed sleepily in the early morning sun, the smoke from their chimneys rising straight into the clear blue of the sky, whilst from behind a group of stately elms, the spire of St. Peter's rose like a silver finger pointing to heaven.

As far as the eye could reach, the rolling downland stretched away to a hazy distance, broken only by an occasional farmhouse nestling in its folds, and the only sounds to break the stillness were the gentle lowing of cattle or the crow of a cock. Even the ruins of Jackson's Folly, bathed in the yellow sunlight, looked less forbidding than usual.

To Roger Marsden, just back from the far East, the whole scene was redolent with the nostalgic charm peculiar to the English countryside and which can be found in no other part of the earth.

Leaning against the old stone balustrade, smoking a pre-breakfast cigarette, he felt at peace with the world. He had good health, a moderate share of good looks, and his prospects were rosy. His sister, Lady Conyers, was devoted to him and it was at her persistent invitation that he had come down to Marbury Court for a protracted visit as soon as he had arrived in England. Only one thing worried him and that was the change in his sister since his return.

Instead of the happy, placid woman he had always known, she now appeared to be anxious and worried, given to fits of melancholy and long periods of brooding silence, when she would sit and stare at nothing, quite oblivious of her surroundings, as though she were waiting for something — something which she dreaded but knew to be inevitable.

In Robert's private opinion, his brother-in-law's behaviour had a great deal to do with this change in his sister. Sir Basil Conyers's chief interest in life was racing, and having in that way managed to dispose of his own fortune, he was now busily engaged in trying to do the same with his wife's. In addition to this, he had an eye for a pretty woman, and was at present behaving with heavy gallantry towards Angela Trevor, Lady Conyers's companion. The girl, it was true, did her best to avoid these advances, but Sir Basil was one of those men who are too thick-skinned to know when his attentions are unwelcome, and too sure of themselves to give up the chase.

There had been an awkward moment on the previous evening. Angela had announced her intention of going for a walk after dinner, and Sir Basil had immediately offered to accompany her. Without being rude, she couldn't very well refuse, but she hadn't liked it and neither had Lady Conyers. She had gone off to her room and Roger had been left to entertain the rest of the house-party,

Mrs. Mortlock, Sir Basil's step-sister, Tony Harper, a cheerful young man who combined the duties of secretary and estate agent. Harper's favourite amusement was dancing attendance on Lady Conyers, who regarded him much in the same way as she might have done a rather trying but well-meaning dog.

The sound of the breakfast gong recalled Roger from his thoughts, and as he turned to go in he encountered Tony Harper as that young man, looking rather tired and dishevelled came running up the steps from the lower lawns.

'Hello,' greeted Roger. 'You're up early.'

'Yes,' replied Harper, with Roger thought a rather overdone casualness, 'I thought I'd like a walk before breakfast.'

They went into the breakfast room where Mrs. Mortlock and Sir Basil were already breakfasting.

''Mornin',' grunted the latter, looking up from his plate. 'Goin' to be a fine day.'

Roger agreed with him and went over and inspected the sideboard. He helped himself to bacon and eggs generously and carried the plate back to the table. Harper seemed to have very little appetite, contenting himself with toast and marmalade. Mrs. Mortlock poured them out coffee.

'Where's Sybil?' asked Roger since there was no sign of his sister.

'Not up yet, I suppose,' grunted her husband, burying his nose in the morning paper. 'One of her headaches, I expect.'

'She ought to do something about those headaches,' remarked Mrs. Mortlock, crumbling her bread. 'You should make her see a doctor, Basil. They're not right for a young woman of her age.'

'Takes too much care of herself as it is,' he retorted. 'If she took a bit more exercise and didn't stay indoors so much, she wouldn't suffer from headaches.' He put down the paper and looked up as the door opened and Angela Trevor came in. 'Here's a girl who's never had a headache in her life, I'll be bound. You don't suffer from headaches, do you, my dear?'

'Sometimes,' said Angela. 'When I do, I go for a long walk. That usually gets rid of it.'

'Exactly what I've just said,' remarked

Sir Basil with great satisfaction.

'Did you get very wet last night, dear?' asked Mrs. Mortlock, as she gave the girl coffee. 'It started to rain again after you and Basil went out.'

'No, I didn't get wet at all,' answered Angela. 'I took shelter.'

Mrs. Mortlock raised her eyebrows and looked at her step-brother.

'Did you take shelter too, Basil?' she asked sweetly.

'No,' he answered. 'I left Angela, or rather she left me, at the bottom of the hill. I turned into the Bull for a drink.'

It all sounded perfectly reasonable but for some reason, Roger didn't believe it. Sir Basil was lying. He might have left Angela at the bottom of the hill, but he *hadn't* gone to the Bull. Probably he was in the middle of some village intrigue as well as chasing his wife's companion.

His speculations concerning the doubtful morals of his brother-in-law were interrupted by the sudden arrival of Lupton, the butler.

'Excuse me, Sir Basil,' he said anxiously, with a worried expression on his usually placid face, 'but there's a police officer to see you, sir . . . '

'A police officer — to see *me*?' echoed Sir Basil in astonishment.

'What have you been up to, Basil?' asked Mrs. Mortlock.

'Nothing — nothing, of course,' snapped Sir Basil, but he looked a little uneasy. 'What does he want, Lupton?'

'He said something about a body, sir,' answered the butler. 'In Jackson's Folly, I think he said . . . '

'A body — in Jackson's Folly?' repeated Sir Basil. 'What the devil's that to do with me?'

The butler shook his grey head.

'I don't know, sir. But the officer wants to see you . . . '

'Show him in here,' he said. 'Good heavens — a body in Jackson's Folly. Some tramp I suppose.'

Tony Harper looked interested.

'Maybe it's a murder,' he said. 'I've always thought that old place would be wonderful for a murder.'

'Oh, don't — don't, please,' broke in Angela, and her face was white.

Lupton returned followed by two men. They were both in plain clothes and obviously nothing to do with the village which boasted only one constable who lived in a small cottage off the High Street. These men, thought Roger, must have come from the neighbouring town of Greystock. Lupton announced them in his best and most majestic manner.

'Inspector Crutchley and Sergeant Trim,' he said and went out closing the door behind him.

The inspector coughed apologetically.

'Sorry to disturb you like this, sir,' he said, 'but there's been a bit of trouble down at the place they call Jackson's Folly. I was wondering if you could help us . . . '

'My butler said something about a body . . . ?' began Sir Basil, and the inspector interrupted him.

'That's right, sir. A man was found dead there this morning. He was killed by a heavy blow on the head.'

'Murder?' exclaimed Tony Harper.

'Well, that's what it appears to be, sir,' answered Inspector Crutchley cautiously.

'We were wondering if, perhaps, someone 'ere may have heard or noticed something during the night?'

There was a general shaking of heads.

'Hardly likely we should see or hear anything,' said Sir Basil. 'Most of the bedrooms are on the other side of the house, you see. With the exception, of course, of my wife's and my own. I always sleep very heavily. Who was the man? Somebody local?'

'He's not been identified yet, sir,' answered the inspector.

'It really is dreadful,' said Mrs. Mortlock. 'So near, too. It's quite frightening.'

'Nothing to be frightened about,' snapped Sir Basil a trifle irritably. 'What was the feller like, eh?'

'Quite an ordinary looking man, sir,' replied the inspector. 'Not very well dressed but not a tramp, if you understand my meaning. He had two or three pounds in notes and some silver in his pocket. It's all rather a queer thing. You don't happen to know whether Lady Conyers was over at Jackson's Folly yesterday at all, do you, sir?'

'My wife?' Sir Basil's tone was astonished. 'Over at Jackson's Folly? Good heavens! Why should she go there?'

'I don't know, sir,' said Inspector Crutchley quietly. 'Perhaps one of these other ladies went there?' He looked at Mrs. Mortlock and Angela.

'It certainly wasn't me!' declared Mrs. Mortlock. 'I went to the village in the morning, but I didn't go anywhere near Jackson's Folly. Miss Trevor went out after dinner last night but I couldn't say where she went!'

'I didn't go anywhere near Jackson's Folly,' said the girl.

'Of course, you didn't,' said Sir Basil. 'What's the idea of these questions, Inspector? You don't imagine that it was one of my household who killed this man, do you?'

'Well, no, sir,' said the inspector awkwardly. 'But you see, we found a scarf — a lady's scarf near the body. It had Lady Conyers' initials on it. Mr. Hornbeam said he'd seen her Ladyship wearing it.'

'A scarf of my wife's,' ejaculated Sir Basil in surprise. 'What the deuce was it doing near the body of this man?'

'That's what we'd like to know, sir,' said the inspector. His tone was respectful but firm. 'I've got the scarf here, sir.'

He turned to the sergeant who had been standing almost at attention throughout the proceedings. Without moving a muscle of his face, Sergeant Trim dived into a cardboard attache-case and, rather in the manner of a conjurer about to produce his best white rabbit, extracted a pink and grey silk square.

Mrs. Mortlock gave an exclamation as soon as she saw it.

'That's Sybil's,' she cried. 'That's her new Jaquemar. She was wearing it yesterday . . . '

'But she never went out,' put in Roger quietly. 'At least only into the garden.'

'That's right,' agreed Sir Basil. 'She didn't.'

'Are you sure this *is* Lady Conyers' scarf, sir?' asked the inspector. 'Perhaps she has more than one of the same kind.'

'Best thing is to ask her,' said Sir Basil.

He got up, went over and rang the bell.

'I'm quite sure she hasn't more than one of that particular pattern,' said Mrs. Mortlock.

'Sybil will know better than anyone else,' remarked Sybil's husband composedly. 'Perhaps she'll be able to account for how it got in Jackson's Folly. She may have lent it to someone.'

'It certainly wasn't me!' declared Mrs. Mortlock quickly. 'I have plenty of scarves of my own.'

Lupton came in with his usual deferential quietness.

'You rang, sir?' he said.

'Will you tell your mistress that I should like to see her as soon as possible,' said Sir Basil.

'Hadn't I better go and explain?' put in Angela, but Sir Basil shook his head.

'No, my dear,' he said. 'You stay where you are. Lupton will see to it.'

The butler withdrew and there was a short silence. Angela fingered her napkin nervously, Tony drummed gently on the table with his finger-tips, Roger stirred his coffee irritably. Only Sir Basil and his step-sister seemed to be quite at ease. Inspector Crutchley was writing something in a notebook, and Sergeant Trim continued to stand at attention and stare fixedly at a portrait of the first Lady Conyers that hung over the mantelpiece as though he were not quite certain that he ought not to arrest her for indecent exposure.

It was Mrs. Mortlock who broke the silence.

'Where did you go last night, dear?' she asked looking across at Angela. 'After you left my step-brother in the village?'

Angela hesitated for a moment before she replied.

'I didn't go anywhere,' she said. 'I just waited for the rain to stop — under the church porch. Then I came home.'

'Then it couldn't have been you I heard coming in late?' said Mrs. Mortlock. 'It must have been you, Basil.'

'Wasn't me,' answered her brother. 'I came straight home from the Bull.'

Roger saw that Inspector Crutchley had pricked up his ears at Mrs. Mortlock's remarks. Was that why the woman had made them, he wondered? There was a distinctly catty element in Mrs. Mortlock's character.

Lupton came back at that moment. His usual manner of quiet deference had been replaced by a certain amount of agitation.

'I'm sorry, sir, but I think her Ladyship is still asleep.' he said. 'I can't make her hear.'

'Did you knock?' asked Sir Basil.

'Yes, sir, several times,' answered Lupton. 'Her ladyship didn't reply. I'd sooner it was washed off before her ladyship sees it. I'm afraid she'll be angry, sir.'

'Washed off — angry?' echoed Sir Basil. 'What on earth are you talking about, Lupton?'

'It's the writing on the door, sir,' said the old man with a troubled expression. 'I told one of the maids to wash it off, sir. I can't imagine who could have done it . . . '

'Done what?' demanded his master in exasperation. 'Don't talk in riddles. What's the matter with the door?'

'If there was a child in the house, sir, I

could understand it,' said Lupton shaking his head. 'None of the staff could have done it. Nursery rhymes — it's like a child, sir . . . '

'Nursery rhymes?' interposed Inspector Crutchley sharply.

'Part of one, sir,' answered the butler. 'It's only one line. In blue pencil or chalk. *This is the cat that killed the rat*. I'm sure it can't be meant to apply to her ladyship, sir,' he added hastily, turning to Sir Basil. 'No one would think of writing such a thing about her.'

3

Miss Titmarsh had a headache. The morning was hot and sultry, and, in spite of the rain on the night before, the air was heavy with the promise of a coming storm.

The children, too, were being more difficult than usual this morning. The news that a body had been discovered in Jackson's Folly, a favourite haunt of theirs, seemed to have completely demoralised them, especially Freddie Suggins who couldn't get over the fact that he had arrived at the spot five minutes after the Reverend Oswald Hornbeam, and been sent post haste down to the village to summon assistance. Five times, Miss Titmarsh had to recall his wandering attention to the tributaries of the Ouse, and even now she could hear his hoarse whisper as he told Myrtle Carp the exact appearance of the dead man.

'Welterin' in 'is gore, 'e was,' he was saying with extreme relish. 'I never see so much blood. Pourin' all over the place, it was, an' drippin' up the stairs . . . '

'Freddie!' said Miss Titmarsh sharply. 'If I hear you talking once more you'll stay in after school and write a hundred lines. You should be ashamed of yourself — trying to frighten Myrtle like that. You know you never saw anything of the kind. And, anyway, blood does *not* drip upwards,' she added turning back to the blackboard.

''Ow do you know, Miss?' said Freddie cheekily. 'You wasn't there. I seen it, an' my mum says I'll 'ave to give evidence at the inquest.'

'Be quiet and get on with your work,' said Miss Titmarsh. She was feeling rather sick now and the room was going round. It would be silly to faint in front of all the children. She pulled herself together and went over to the window. Perhaps a little air would make her feel better and ease the throbbing in her head.

As she stood listlessly gazing out while the class struggled to draw a map of the

Ouse from memory, she suddenly saw the Reverend Oswald Hornbeam hurrying toward the school-house. He was without a hat and his white hair stood out around his head like a halo. Miss Titmarsh watched him with interest. A fine figure of a man, she thought, so noble and saintly. It must have been a terribly experience for him finding a body at Jackson's Folly.

Mr. Hornbeam certainly looked paler than usual and his face wore a worried expression. Just as he reached the school-house gate, Major Panting appeared coming from the opposite direction. Miss Titmarsh's face hardened. She disliked Major Panting. But the rector was obviously glad to see him. He almost ran towards him.

Miss Titmarsh gently lowered the window a little more. They were together now, and the rector was talking voluably. Major Panting appeared to be shocked and horrified by what he was saying.

Miss Titmarsh leaned out over the window. Unfortunately she could hear very little, the wind was in the wrong direction and she could only catch an occasional word or two. She leaned further out to hear better and suddenly became conscious of heavy breathing at her side. Turning her head she saw the shiny, excited face of Freddie Suggins grinning up at her.

'Little pitchers 'as big ears,' he remarked conversationally.

Miss Titmarsh felt herself going crimson. She opened her mouth to retort sharply, when the church clock began to strike twelve. With a sound like a tidal wave the entire class rose as one. Their boots thudded and clattered as they fought their way to the door with frenzied cries of delight at the prospect of freedom from the tributaries of the Ouse. For a few seconds pandemonium reigned and then there was a complete stillness as their shrill voices faded away in the distance.

Miss Titmarsh knew she should have stopped them. She should have called them back and made them leave the classroom properly and quietly. She should have read them a lecture on behaviour and kept them for an extra five minutes. She knew she should have done all these things but she wasn't feeling well and she was curious. She saw the children streaming up the hill towards Jackson's Folly led by the irrepressible Freddie Suggins, and turning away from the window, pinned on her hat with trembling fingers. If she hurried she might be in time to catch the rector.

Perhaps Major Panting would have gone by then. There was something about Major Panting that had always repelled her — something cold and calculating. He would watch her while he was talking, his little pale blue eyes never leaving her face and never blinking, a curious mocking little smile on his fat, red face. Like a snake, she thought, a snake watching a rabbit . . .

She shuddered slightly as she drew on her gloves. It felt cold in the schoolroom now. Really, there must be something seriously the matter with her to feel cold on a day like this. Perhaps she was in for a touch of flu. She hoped not. It would be very inconvenient at a time like this — with all the examination papers to correct. Just a little quinine, perhaps, when she got home. Luckily it was Wednesday and a half-holiday. She would lie down on the sitting room sofa with the blinds drawn . . .

She picked up a bundle of exercise books and walked to the door. Outside, the rector and Major Panting were still talking to one another. For a moment they did not appear to notice Miss Titmarsh, then the major saw her and raised his hat politely.

'Ah, Miss Titmarsh,' he said. 'Have you heard this very sad news?'

'You mean — about the man?' she began but the major shook his head.

'No, indeed,' interpolated Mr. Hornbeam gravely. 'Poor Lady Conyers . . . '

'Lady Conyers?' echoed Miss Titmarsh. 'What's the matter with Lady Conyers?'

'She's dead,' answered the major. 'Terrible, isn't it?'

His small eyes stared at her as usual, boring into her mind, or so it seemed to Miss Titmarsh.

'Poor, poor, woman,' said the rector gently. 'She was found dead in her bed. I can hardly believe it, but it's true, I'm afraid.'

'Dead?' repeated Miss Titmarsh, thoroughly shocked. 'Oh no — It can't be possible.'

'It is, all the same,' declared Major Panting with a hint of relish in his voice. 'The police are at the Court now.'

Miss Titmarsh looked at him with horrified eyes.

'You don't mean — that she — she took her own life?' she almost whispered.

'I'm quite sure she didn't,' declared the rector stoutly. 'Lady Conyers would never be guilty of that — no matter under what provocation. She was a good Christian lady. Such a thing would be against all her principles.'

'Well, that only leaves two possibilities,' remarked the major reflectively. 'Either an accident — or murder.'

'Oh, it couldn't be murder, surely?' exclaimed Miss Titmarsh. 'Not another. One was enough . . . ' She stopped abruptly and her eyes filled with tears.

'Dear Miss Titmarsh, don't distress yourself,' said the rector kindly. 'It must be a terrible shock to you — as indeed it is to all of us — but you are in no way to blame, you know.' He patted her shoulder gently and the major eyed her keenly.

'What did you mean by 'one was enough', Miss Titmarsh?' he said. 'You don't think these deaths were connected, do you?'

'No — no, of course not. That would be impossible, wouldn't it?' she said a little incoherently. She replaced a strand of hair that had escaped from under her hat, with a shaking hand. 'These things are so terrible when they happen,' she went inconsequently. 'One doesn't know *what* to think . . . '

The rector shook his head sadly.

'It's all very disturbing,' he said. 'I don't understand it. This poor lady might have taken an overdose of some sleeping drug — I gather it was something of the sort that caused her death — or . . . ' He stopped and shook his head again.

'Or she might have been given it, eh?' finished the major. 'Well, it's no use conjecturing until we know the full facts. Are you going up to Marbury Court,

Rector? If you are, I'll walk part of the way with you.'

The Reverend Oswald Hornbeam was obviously uncertain what to do.

'I suppose, I ought to call and offer my condolences,' he said doubtfully. 'Really, it's very difficult to know what to do for the best. What can one say under the circumstances? It's not always easy to do the right thing . . . '

'No — very awkward for you,' said Major Panting sympathetically. 'You fellers always have the unpleasant jobs in cases like this . . . '

'I just can't believe that it's really happened,' declared Miss Titmarsh plaintively. 'Such terrible things — in our little community . . . They really seem impossible . . . '

'Yes, yes, I know how you feel,' said the rector staring abstractedly at the sky. 'First that poor fellow at Jackson's Folly, and now this tragedy at the Court. Dreadful, dreadful.'

'You surely don't connect them in anyway?' said Major Panting.

The Reverend Oswald Hornbeam looked

at him with a suddenly startled expression on his mild face.

'Good gracious, my dear fellow, of course not! I was only saying . . .'

'I must be getting along to luncheon,' said Miss Titmarsh. 'A very frugal meal. One has no appetite this sultry weather . . .'

'I can always manage a good steak, myself,' remarked the major, and Miss Titmarsh gave a delicate shudder. 'Nothing like a good steak. Puts new life in you.'

Miss Titmarsh looked as if she could do with 'new life'. Her thin face was drawn and pasty as she wished them 'goodbye' and tripped away.

Major Panting stared after her retreating figure with his small eyes almost closed.

'Never did like that woman,' he remarked. 'Don't trust her, somehow. If she gave someone a dose of arsenic one day it'ud never surprise me . . .'

The rector smiled.

'She's very conscientious,' he said non-committally.

'Remember all that fuss she made about the drawing?' asked the major. 'Accused me — *me*! As if I'd waste my time drawing a picture of the old scarecrow . . . Did you see it, by the way?'

The rector shook his head and the major chuckled reminiscently.

'It was damn good, whoever did it,' he said. 'They used a blue pencil and her nose was really a work of art — drop at the end and all. You know how she looks on a cold day?'

'If I'm going up to Marbury Court before luncheon,' said the rector, changing the subject. 'I'd better be on my way. Are you walking with me?'

It was pretty clear that he would much rather Major Panting did not, but he was disappointed. The major agreed with alacrity and they started to walk up the hill together. For a few minutes neither of them spoke and finally it was the Reverend Oswald who broke the silence.

'You know,' he said hesitantly, 'I can't help feeling that something unpleasant is happening — something that will destroy the peace of our little village.'

'I should say enough has happened to do that already,' remarked Major Panting.

'I don't think you quite understand what I mean,' said the rector. 'It may be imagination, but I am conscious of a sense of evil. It seems to me to be in the very air. I have a premonition that something evil has been loosed among us . . .'

'What you want is a good stiff whisky,' retorted the major. 'Come along to my place and I'll give you four fingers of Johnny Walker. That'll pull you up. Soon settle your nerves.'

'No, no, thank you,' replied Mr. Hornbeam. 'I like my little nightcap, but not in the day time. I'm a trifle tired that's all. I must be getting old.'

'We're all getting old,' said Major Panting. 'The only thing most of us have to look forward to these days is getting old peacefully and dying comfortably in our beds. The trouble is, we don't know what's in store for any of us.'

'No,' said the rector thoughtfully, 'we don't know what's in store. Perhaps,' he added, 'that is just as well.'

4

Miss Titmarsh ate her frugal luncheon — which wasn't so very frugal after all, consisting of a large chop, tinned peas and potatoes, followed by canned peaches and cream — washed up the dishes, looked round her neat kitchen to make sure that everything was in its proper place, and went through into her little sitting room.

She felt better now. Her headache had almost gone. Food, she decided was what she had needed. Now, after a short rest, she ought to feel quite well again.

She drew the curtains over the window to shut out the light, adjusted a slightly crooked photograph of herself as captain of the school hockey team, and decorously laid herself down on the old horse-hair sofa to rest.

She closed her eyes and tried to compose herself for sleep, but sleep would not come so easily. Her brain refused to relax. A confused jumble of impressions and events crowded through her mind — vague nightmares all tending toward one focal point, the one thing she was trying so hard to forget.

She felt, after a little while, that her headache was returning — coming back with little stabs of pain until her whole head was throbbing. She must do something to relieve it. If it continued she would go mad.

She got up, went into the microscopic bathroom, took some aspirin and bathed her forehead. Then she made herself a strong cup of tea and began to feel a little better.

It was no use worrying. Unless she did something foolish nobody would ever find out. But she must be very careful. It was so necessary not to make a mistake after all these years. What was done was done and nothing could alter it. That reminded her. There *was* something that had to be done, and done at once.

She went over to the small bureau in the corner of the sitting room, sat down and opened an exercise book.

Then she selected a blue pencil and began to write . . .

* * *

The saloon bar of the Bull was crowded. It didn't require any considerable number of people to achieve this result for the bar was extremely small — a room that had been converted from the original bar-parlour when the Bull was only an ale-house, frequented solely by farm-hands and labourers.

The sole topic of conversation seemed to consist of the tragic death of Lady Conyers and the discovery of the dead man in Jackson's Folly. In that incredibly swift way that things have a habit of leaking out in an English village, the nursery rhyme on Lady Conyers' door and the other portion of it pinned on the door of Jackson's Folly, had become common property and there was much discussion concerning it.

It had taken hold of peoples imagination and lifted the whole thing into the category of the sensational story.

Inspector Crutchley, making himself as inconspicuous as possible in a dark corner of the bar, sipped his pint of draught beer and listened to the various comments that were being made, but if he had ever hoped to pick up anything useful, he soon came to the conclusion that his hope was in vain.

Most of them were repetition interspersed with several wild and completely impossible theories that had neither facts nor plausibility to recommend them.

The inspector was not feeling very happy about the matter. It was something quite out of his normal sphere, and he had not made a great deal of headway. The identity of the dead man still remained unknown. There was nothing in his pockets to say who he was or where he came from. Crutchley had taken the precaution, however, of taking his fingerprints and sending specimens of them to Scotland Yard. He wasn't very sanguine that this would achieve any result but it was a matter of routine. It was to have very far reaching results, but he couldn't foresee that at the moment.

The thing that worried him and appeared to be the greatest puzzle of the whole case was the death of Lady Conyers and the obvious connection between it and the murder at Jackson's Folly. The doctor's examination of the dead woman had definitely precluded the possibility of accident. She had not died from an overdose of sleeping pills or anything of that kind. She had died from poison — cyanide of potassium. Traces had still remained in a glass of water on her bedside table. She might have taken it deliberately or she might not. If not, then this was another murder.

Inspector Crutchley was of the opinion that it was. Otherwise how could the nursery rhyme written on the door of her bedroom be accounted for? It was hardly likely that the dead woman, if she had committed suicide, would have scrawled it there. And it linked up with the other part of the same rhyme on the paper pinned to the door of Jackson's Folly. There must definitely be a connection between the two deaths, though 'what' and 'how' was beyond Inspector Crutchley's imagination. Her ladyship had apparently been to the ruined house, or someone had taken her scarf there . . .

It was all very curious and very perplexing. What exactly was the reason for the nursery rhyme? Memories of his childhood came back to Inspector Crutchley. His lips moved silently as he repeated to himself the old rhyme which he had heard at his mother's knee.

'This is the house that Jack built.
'This is the Malt that lay in the
   house that Jack built.
'This is the Rat that ate the Malt
   that lay in the house that Jack
   built.
'This is the Cat that killed the Rat
   that ate the Malt that lay in the
   house that Jack built.
'This is the Dog that worried the
   Cat that killed the Rat that ate
   the Malt that lay in the house
   that Jack built.
'This is the Cow with a crumpled
   horn that tossed the Dog that
   worried the Cat that killed the
   Rat that ate the Malt that lay in

the house that Jack built.
'This is the Maiden all forlorn who
milked the Cow with the
crumpled horn that tossed the
Dog that worried the Cat that
killed the Rat that ate the Malt
that lay in the house that Jack
built.
'This is the Man all tattered and
torn who kissed the Maiden all
forlorn who milked the Cow with
the crumpled horn that tossed the
Dog that worried the Cat that
killed the Rat that ate the Malt
that lay in the house that Jack
built.
'This is the Priest all shaven and
shorn who married the Man all
tattered and torn who kissed the
Maiden all forlorn who milked
the Cow with the crumpled horn
that tossed the Dog that worried
the Cat that killed the Rat that
ate the Malt that lay in the house
that Jack built.
'This is the Cock that crowed in the
Morn that waked the Priest all

*shaven and shorn who married
the Man all tattered and torn who
kissed the Maiden all forlorn who
milked the Cow with the
crumpled horn that tossed the
Dog that worried the Cat that
killed the Rat that ate the Malt
that lay in the house that Jack
built.'*

That was all the inspector could remember. He thought that was the lot. It wasn't very illuminating as regards throwing any light on the reason for writing those bits of it on the doors. And yet the person who had done it must have *had* a reason. Blue pencil in both cases, too. Did *that* mean anything?

Inspector Crutchley shook his head slowly. He couldn't see any reason in any of it. Here was an unknown man bludgeoned to death in an empty house, and a highly respectable lady poisoned in her bedroom. There was some connection between these two incidents, but what? Of course, they hadn't got all the facts yet. Perhaps there was something in Lady

51

Conyers' life that linked her with the thin-faced little man in Jackson's Folly. Maybe, that would come out during the inquiry. '*This is the rat that ate the malt that lay in the house that Jack built*.' The dead man hadn't been unlike a rat, either. What was the malt he was supposed to have eaten? Was there something there? According to the other part of the rhyme on Lady Conyers' door, it was she who killed him. '*This is the cat that killed the rat*.' That might be true, but who had killed *her*? Or had she killed herself? Again the inspector's head moved slowly from side to side. He didn't think she had. In his opinion it was the same person who had killed both the little man in Jackson's Folly *and* Lady Conyers and for some reason best known to himself, or herself, had left the scrawled rhymes behind . . .

Inspector Crutchley sighed. It was a puzzling business and no mistake. There'd have to be two inquests and they'd cause a lot of stir in the neighbourhood. Both 'ud probably have to be adjourned. He finished the remainder of his beer and left the Bull a little dispirited. It had been a long and weary day and he hadn't got very much to show for his labours. Certainly nothing much to report to the Chief Constable with whom he had an appointment on the following morning.

★ ★ ★

Colonel Blair, the Assistant Commissioner for the Criminal Investigation Department at New Scotland Yard, finished reading the letter and its accompanying report, pushed it away from him, leaned back in his chair, and smoothed his neat grey hair with a well-kept hand. There was a slight frown on his face which cleared after a moment as he stretched out his hand for the house telephone and, lifting the receiver, gave an extension number.

'Is that you, Superintendent?' he asked when he was put through. 'Come along to my office at once, will you please.'

At the other end of the line, Mr. Budd put down the receiver, looked across at Sergeant Leek who was laboriously writing in a tattered exercise book, and sighed.

'No rest for the wicked,' he grunted. 'Blair wants me.'

The sergeant raised his eyes and his lean face lengthened.

'I 'ope it ain't nothin' that's goin' to be difficult,' he said.

'What difference will it make to you?' demanded Mr. Budd as he hoisted himself with difficulty out of his chair. 'You never do anything anyway. What's all that you're scribbling?'

The melancholy sergeant's eyes brightened.

'I'm making notes fer me autobiography,' he said.

'Your *what?*' snorted Mr. Budd.

'Me autobiography,' answered Leek proudly. 'I'm goin' to write me reminiscences. They'll be sensational.'

'They won't be very long, anyway,' grunted his superior. 'You've never been awake long enough to have many!'

He lumbered out of the office and made his way to the assistant commissioner's room.

'Sit down, Superintendent,' said Colonel Blair, and when the stout man had lowered himself carefully into a chair: 'I've had a request from the chief constable of Blankshire for assistance.' He tapped the letter that lay on the desk before him. 'There's been a murder and a death at a place called Marbury under peculiar circumstances — very peculiar circumstances,' he added.

'A murder *and* a death?' repeated Mr. Budd questioningly.

Colonel Blair smiled.

'Yes,' he answered. 'There's no doubt the one was murder but they're not quite sure about the other. It could be suicide.'

'I see, sir,' said Mr. Budd sleepily. 'What are the peculiar circumstances?'

'I've only the barest details here,' said the assistant commissioner. 'Apparently there's a nursery rhyme mixed up in it. The murder took place at a place called Jackson's Folly, an old ruined house in the neighbourhood, and there was a bit out of '*The House that Jack Built*' scrawled on a page from an exercise book in blue pencil and pinned on the door . . . '

He related the discovery made by the Reverend Oswald Hornbeam on the morning he had gone forth in search of mushrooms.

'That's not all,' he continued. 'There was another part of the same rhyme written, again in blue pencil, on the bedroom door of the woman who died, Lady Conyers. She was either poisoned with cyanide of potassium by someone, or she took the stuff herself.'

'Suicide?' remarked the superintendent and Colonel Blair nodded.

'The police think it was murder, too,' he said, 'but they're not sure. Apparently this woman was a big bug in the district, wife of Sir Basil Conyers, old family, dates back to 1672. It's because of that that the chief constable has asked for our help. He's a bit scared of making any mistakes. If there are any mistakes made, the Yard will take the can back.'

'Who was the dead man, sir?' asked Mr. Budd. 'Was he a member of an old family too?'

Colonel Blair chuckled.

'Yes, in a way,' he said. 'One of the old family of crooks! The local police sent along his fingerprints and we checked up on 'em. Sam Sprigot known, I believe, as 'Stackpipe Sam'.'

'That the feller, eh?' remarked Mr. Budd. 'Now fancy Sam getting himself murdered. He only came out o' prison a few months ago.'

'That's the man,' said Colonel Blair. 'We've traced him up.' He pulled a sheet of paper toward him on which were some scrawled notes. 'He was staying in lodgings at 15 Tight Street, at the back of the Waterloo Road. A Mrs. Bagley's the landlady. That's about all I can tell you. You'd better get off to this place Marbury as soon as you can. Report to Superintendent Sones at Greystock, that's the nearest town to Marbury. He's in charge. He'll probably be able to give you more details.'

He nodded a dismissal and Mr. Budd left the office and betook himself wearily back to his own.

'You can forget your autobiography for

a bit an' do a little honest work,' he remarked to Leek as he came in. 'We've got an inquiry. We're goin' to Marbury to look at some nursery rhymes.'

Leek's long face looked surprised.

'I don't suppose you ever knew any nursery rhymes,' said Mr. Budd, taking one of his evil-looking black cigars from his pocket and sniffing at it with great enjoyment. 'I can't imagine you as a baby.'

'My mother thought I was a beautiful baby,' said Leek. 'All our relations used ter come miles ter have a look at me.'

'People do that to the freaks in the circus,' said Mr. Budd rudely. 'Have you ever heard of the House that Jack built?'

'Of course, I 'ave,' said the sergeant. ' "This is the house that Jack built. This is the malt that lay in the house that Jack built. This is the rat that ate the malt that lay in . . . " '

'All right, all right, that'll do,' interrupted the big man. 'I didn't ask you to recite. You better get ready to come with me. Somebody's killed the rat that ate the malt an' were going to find out who it is.'

5

Mr. Budd and Sergeant Leek arrived at Greystock shortly after five-thirty. They found Superintendent Sones, a short, stout, ginger-haired man with a pleasant smile, waiting for them at the police station. He had arranged lodgings for them both at a farm on the outskirts of Marbury. Before taking them there, it was decided that they should have a conference to which Inspector Crutchley was invited.

'It's a very queer business,' said Superintendent Sones, scratching gently at his short, ginger moustache, a habit which they discovered later was habitual with him when he was worried. 'I'm very glad to have your help, I don't mind admitting. Now, I'll get Crutchley, here, to go over all he's got so far. It isn't much I'm afraid.'

It wasn't much. It turned out to be very little more than Mr. Budd had already learned from the assistant commissioner. But he was able to add a small item of information to their meagre stock of knowledge.

Before leaving for Greystock, he had paid a visit to Mrs. Bagley and had learned from that interested woman about the letter which Sam Sprigot had received on the morning before his death.

'This woman says it gave him a shock,' said Mr. Budd. 'Accordin' to her, it was a pretty bad one too. It was the only letter he had while he was lodging with 'er.'

'She didn't notice the post-mark, I suppose?' asked Sones, and Mr. Budd shook his head.

'No,' he answered regretfully. 'It was smudged. But the envelope was an expensive kind. Not the kind of envelope any friends o' Sam's would be likely to use. We searched his luggage, which he'd left behind, there was only one rather battered old suitcase, but we didn't find anythin'. Only a few personal belongings.'

'It looks as though he was expecting to go back,' remarked Inspector Crutchley.

'Leaving his luggage there.'

'Yes, I think he was expectin' to go back,' agreed Mr. Budd. 'I should say that that letter was some sort of an appointment — to meet somebody. An' judgin' by what this woman says, he was a bit scared . . . '

'Not without reason, as it turned out,' grunted Sones. 'The appointment was made at Jackson's Folly, I suppose?'

'Either that, or he was brought there,' said the stout superintendent.

'He came to Marbury by himself,' put in Crutchley. 'I made inquiries at the station. The porter remembers 'im getting out of the train. It was the last one, an' 'e was the only passenger to get out.'

'Queer sort of place to make an appointment at,' remarked Sones. 'In the middle of the night too. You'd think, if he was scared of the person he was going to meet, he wouldn't have kept it.'

'Maybe 'e had to,' said Mr. Budd. 'We're only conjecturing that this letter he got was makin' an appointment. It may've been somethin' else, altogether.'

'Well, he met somebody,' said Sones,

'and there must have been an arrangement for the meeting, so I should say we could take it that it was in the latter.'

'An' the person he met, if you take the evidence of that scarf,' said Crutchley, 'was Lady Conyers.'

'I can't believe there could have been anything between a chap like this feller, Sprigot, an' a lady like Lady Conyers,' said Superintendent Sones, shaking his red head. 'What could she have wanted to meet him for? Besides, can you imagine a woman dealing a blow like the one that killed him? Smashed his head in like pulp. It wanted a good bit of strength to do that.'

'And from the look of things,' remarked Mr. Budd thoughtfully, 'someone killed Lady Conyers. If it wasn't suicide,' he added.

'I'm quite sure it wasn't suicide,' declared Sones.

'Which means it must have been an inside job,' said the stout superintendent. 'How exactly did it happen?'

Crutchley cleared his throat.

'Lady Conyers was in the habit of

taking a sleeping tablet every night,' he replied. 'The tablets were kept in a bottle on her bedside table, and a fresh glass of water was left beside them last thing at night by the maid . . . '

'And after her death, this glass of water was found to contain traces of cyanide,' interposed Sones. 'She'd taken her sleeping tablet and swallowed it down with water from the glass . . . '

'How d'you know she took a sleeping tablet?' interjected Mr. Budd quickly.

'She used to get them in bottles of twenty-five at a time,' answered Crutchley. 'This was a new bottle. There were only twenty-four tablets in it left.'

Mr. Budd nodded approvingly.

'I see,' he said. 'So somebody popped some cyanide in the glass of water, knowin' she was bound to drink some of it. Simple.'

'But who?' demanded Sones. 'And why?'

'We haven't collected enough facts to answer that one,' said Mr. Budd. 'What I'm interested in are these bits of rhymes. There was one on the door o' this place

Jackson's Folly, an' there was another on the door of Lady Conyers' bedroom. Now, the question is: why was they put there? Was it just a queer bit o' humour on the part of the murderer, or is there some reason — some sensible reason for it?'

'If you can think of one, you're a cleverer man than I am,' declared Sones.

Mr. Budd leaned back in his chair which creaked protestingly under his weight. He looked with sleepy, half-closed eyes at a corner of the desk.

' "This is the house that Jack built",' he murmured softly. ' "This is the Malt that lay in the house that Jack built. This is the Rat that ate the Malt that lay in the house that Jack built. This is the Cat that killed the Rat that ate the Malt that lay in the house that Jack built.' H'm, that's as far as we've got at present. Do you find anything suggestive in that?'

They stared at him blankly.

'You don't, eh?' went on Mr. Budd. He shrugged his broad shoulders. 'Oh well, perhaps you're right. Maybe I'm just imaginin' things. It's only an idea

— prob'ly the wrong one.' He changed the subject abruptly before they could ask him what he meant. 'Who was this feller, Jackson?'

'You mean the chap who built the Folly?' asked Sones unnecessarily. 'Well, he's dead. He died a good many years ago . . . '

'Over fifty,' said Inspector Crutchley. 'He's got nothing to do with this business.'

'Maybe not,' said Mr. Budd. He yawned. 'Who does the place belong to now?'

Sones shook his head.

'Can't tell you that,' he answered. 'It's been a ruin as long as I can remember. I suppose it must belong to somebody but they don't come near it. Why do you want to know?'

'Just curiosity,' said Mr. Budd sleepily. 'I've got a very strongly developed bump o' curiosity. I think, if you don't mind, we'll go along to these digs you've got for us, have a bit of grub, an' then I'd like to meet the people at Marbury Court.'

Superintendent Sones was in agreement with this programme. He sent for a police car and drove with them to a charming old farmhouse set in a country lane within a quarter of a mile of the village of Marbury. Mr. and Mrs. Kenwiddy, the elderly couple to whom the farm belonged, welcomed them with a friendliness that made them feel instantly at home, showed them to two delightful rooms under the thatched eaves, and declared that a meal would be ready for them in a few minutes.

As soon as he had seen them fixed up, Superintendent Sones took his departure, arranging for Inspector Crutchley to meet them at the farm in two hours time.

Mr. Budd unpacked his bag, had a wash, and went down to find the most enormous meal he had ever seen spread out on a large table in the sitting room.

Sergeant Leek's eyes glistened when he came in a few minutes later and saw what had been prepared for them.

'Do yer well, don't they?' he said as he drew up a chair and sat down.

'Don't forget to mention it in your reminiscences,' said Mr. Budd. 'It'll probably be the only interestin' bit in the book.'

When he had finished, he left Leek dozing in an easy chair, and lighting one of his black, evil-smelling cigars, went in search of Mr. Kenwiddy and information.

Mr. Kenwiddy, a small, gnarled man with yellowish-white hair and the skin which goes with a long life in close contact with the soil, listened to what he had to say and nodded.

'Aye,' he said. 'I know all about Jackson's Folly. So do the wife. We was little childers when William Jackson built the place. Now, let me see, that'ud be over sixty year ago, that'ud be. A rare bit o' trouble it caused.'

'Trouble?' said Mr. Budd.

'Aye, with the Conyers at Marbury Court,' answered Mr. Kenwiddy. 'That'ud be the present Sir Basil's father, o' course.' He chuckled with a rattling hoarseness. ''E didn't want a 'ouse there at all, yer see. Swore it'ud spoil the view from 'is terrace. But 'e couldn't do nuthin' about it, though it weren't fer want o' tryin'. Jackson 'ad bought the land and nobody could stop 'im buildin' 'is house. It didn't do 'im much good, though, it didn't.'

'What happened?' prompted Mr. Budd.

'When they built the well for the water,' said Mr. Kenwiddy, 'they built it too near the cess-pit. There weren't no other water supply, you see, or sanitation. The cons'quence was the water got pizoned. There was a seepage inter the well from the pit, yer see. Mrs. Jackson was took ill an' died an' so did the child. O' course, arter that, William Jackson wouldn't live there no more an' no one 'ud buy it 'cos it would've cost too much money to put in a main water supply. He died himself soon arter.'

'An' the house just fell into a ruin, I suppose?' said the stout man.

Mr. Kenwiddy nodded.

'Yes,' he said. 'The kids in the neighbourhood used ter play around there. They kept to the garden at first but arter a bit the winders got broke an' gradual like the 'ole place fell to bits. Like it is now.'

'Who owns it now?' asked Mr. Budd.

But Mr. Kenwiddy was not in a position to answer this. He supposed that it must belong to somebody, but he couldn't say who.

It would seem, thought Mr. Budd, that the original Jackson or his descendents could have nothing to do with the present mystery. But he was glad he had found out the story that lay behind the Folly. He had a tidy mind and he liked to clear things up as he went along. He had wondered why the house had been allowed to go to rack and ruin, and now he knew. A certain vague idea that lay at the back of his mind had not been altered by what he had learned.

If there was reason to the rhyme that loomed so largely in this queer business, he thought, as he returned to the slumbering Leek, that vague idea might very well turn out to be true.

6

The death of Lady Conyers had, not unnaturally, brought an atmosphere of gloom to Marbury Court.

Sir Basil, for perhaps the first time in his life, was uninterested in either horses or women, and spent his time moodily walking about the grounds or shut up in the library. Angela, who had been really fond of the dead woman, was silent, going about the house with a pale face and swollen eyelids, and avoiding the rest of the household as much as she could. Tony Harper, immersed himself in his estate duties and was only seen at meal times, during which he said very little, keeping his eyes fixed on his plate. Even Mrs. Mortlock's acid tongue was less in evidence than usual although she couldn't refrain from an occasional spiteful remark from pure force of habit.

Roger Marsden, smoking his pipe on the terrace, wore a puzzled frown. He and his sister had been genuinely devoted to each other and the shock of her sudden death had been such a paralizing shock to him that his senses were still numb. He remembered the change he had noticed in her and wondered more than once since the tragedy, what had been the cause.

He wished now, fervently, that he had asked her what the matter was, but he had put it down to the behaviour of her husband and hadn't liked to interfere. That it was not due to Sir Basil's behaviour, he was pretty sure. There had been something else — some secret that had been the cause of the anxiety he had seen in her eyes and those fits of melancholy and brooding silence. And it was something she had been either ashamed of, or too afraid of, to tell him.

If it had been anything more or less ordinary, she would have confided in him at once, he was sure of that. They had shared their troubles when they were children, and they had gone on sharing them in later life until she had married Sir Basil Conyers, and he, Roger, had joined the R.A.F. in the war. And this secret of hers, whatever it had been had led to her death.

Roger was under no delusions about that death being anything else but murder. He knew his sister well enough to be certain that under no circumstances whatever would she take her own life. She had been deliberately killed because of what she knew — because of this secret that she had been so closely guarding.

Roger tapped the ashes out of his pipe, put it in his pocket, and lighted a cigarette. There was a connection somehow between the man who had been killed in Jackson's Folly and this secret which had been worrying his sister. Had she been in the old house when he was killed? Had she seen the murder committed and was that why she had had to die too? Her scarf had been found there and, so far as Roger could see, no one else could have taken it. It would have been easy for her to slip out of the house after they had all gone to bed . . .

But *why?* That was the crux of it. *Why?* Why should a woman like Sybil sneak out of her own house to go and meet a man like that in the middle of the night?

And why choose a place like Jackson's Folly, falling to pieces and overrun with rats, as a meeting place? Or hadn't she any choice in that?

Roger shook his head unconsciously.

It wasn't very much use conjecturing. He hadn't enough facts to come to any decision. But he was determined to get to the bottom of it if it took him the rest of his life. If only Sybil had confided in him. She ought to have known that she could rely on him whatever the trouble was . . .

Well, it was too late now . . .

He flung away the remainder of his cigarette and turned to go in just as Lupton came out onto the terrace through the open windows of the drawing room. The old man looked worried and drawn.

'Inspector Crutchley is here with two other men, sir,' said the old butler. 'Two detectives from London. I can't find Sir Basil anywhere . . . '

'I'll see them,' said Roger. 'Where are they?'

'In the library, sir,' answered Lupton. 'I thought Sir Basil was there. The last time I saw him he was just going into the library. He must have gone out . . . '

So the local police had called in Scotland Yard, thought Roger, as he followed the butler into the house. That was a good thing. Perhaps they'd get to the truth of the matter. The local people didn't seem to have made much head-way . . .

Inspector Crutchley, Mr. Budd, and Sergeant Leek were standing in a little group in front of the big fireplace when Roger came in, and Inspector Crutchley effected the necessary introductions.

'The Superintendent would like to have a word with Sir Basil and the rest of the household,' he concluded, 'but it seems that Sir Basil can't be found at the moment . . . '

'Mr. Marsden 'ull do to be goin' on with,' interposed Mr. Budd in his slow and rather ponderous manner. 'Maybe, by the time we get through with Mr. Marsden an' some o' the other people, Sir Basil will turn up. You were the dead lady's brother, I understand, sir?'

Roger nodded.

'Very nasty thing for you,' said Mr. Budd sympathetically. 'Very unpleasant for everybody, but especially for you, sir . . .'

'Even more unpleasant for my sister,' said Roger shortly.

'That's true enough,' agreed Mr. Budd. 'Unfortunately we can't do much about that, you see. All we can do is to try an' find out who was responsible for her death . . .'

'I shall be satisfied if you do that,' retorted Roger. 'I'm glad you've given up the idea that it was suicide . . .'

'Well, we haven't actually given it up,' remarked Mr. Budd gently. 'We can't neglect the possibility until we've proved it to be wrong. Let's say that the probabilities point to its *not* havin' been suicide.'

He scratched the lowest of his many chins and pursed up his lips.

Roger was not impressed. It seemed to him that this stout, sleepy-eyed man, who spoke so slowly and deliberately, was unlikely to be much good at discovering anything. A very large number of people had suffered under the same delusion.

'What do you want to ask me?' he demanded curtly.

Mr. Budd regarded him through half-closed eyes. He was perfectly well aware what he was thinking. He had seen the same expression so often before and it invariably gave him a great deal of inward amusement. He had also found it invaluable in the past, to create just this impression on people. They were so very apt, to their cost sometimes, to underestimate the quickness of the brain behind that lethargic exterior.

'Well, sir,' he said after a pause. 'I'd like to hear your account of your sister's movements on the day prior to her death. Was she in her usual spirits? Did she seem to have somethin' on her mind? Did she have any letters or telephone calls that mornin' or durin' the day? Just tell me everythin' you can remember. Don't try an' pick out the things *you* think might be important. You can leave me to sort them out. Just give me the lot, sir.'

Roger gave him the lot. And when it was all said and done it amounted to very little. Sybil had spent that last day very much like any other. She hadn't gone out except for a brief walk in the garden. She hadn't had any letters, at least not to his knowledge, or any telephone calls, again as far as he knew. She had certainly seemed worried and dispirited, but then that had been her normal state recently. Roger explained that he had found this change in her when he had returned from abroad.

Mr. Budd listened quietly until Roger had finished. Then he said: 'And you had no idea of anythin' that would account for this change in your sister, sir?'

Roger hesitated for a moment.

'I thought it was due to her husband's behaviour,' he said, and explained Sir Basil's addiction to horse-racing and pretty women. 'I'm quite sure I was wrong, now,' he ended. 'There was something else.'

Mr. Budd nodded.

'I think you're prob'ly right,' he said. 'I believe, Lady Conyers retired early that night?'

'Yes,' answered Roger. 'Very soon after dinner.'

'An' nobody saw her after that until her body was found in the mornin'?'

'So far as I know that is correct.'

Mr. Budd continued to scratch his chin.

'There's nothin' you heard, or noticed, that night that 'ud be likely to help us?' he asked after a pause, and Roger shook his head.

'If there had been I should have mentioned it before,' he said.

'Ah — yes, no doubt you would,' remarked Mr. Budd staring up at a corner of the ceiling. 'Of course, you would. Well, I think that will be all for the moment, Mr. Marsden. Perhaps you'd ask one of the other people here to step in?'

Roger nodded.

'Any one in particular?' he inquired.

'No — no, just as they happen to be available,' said Mr. Budd helpfully. 'I'll be seein' 'em all, so it don't matter in what order.'

'We've been over all this, you know,' remarked Inspector Crutchley when Roger had gone.

'Yes, yes, I know,' agreed the stout superintendent. 'But I like to get these things first hand, if you know what I mean?'

The inspector looked as if he not only knew what he meant but privately thought that the whole thing was a waste of time. If this, he thought, was the way Scotland Yard went about things, it was a wonder to him how it ever got any results at all.

Mrs. Mortlock came in. She came in very quickly, and there was almost an eager light in her eyes as they swept over the little group by the fireplace.

'This is a terrible affair — terrible,' she said breathlessly. 'It's been a great shock to us all, especially my poor step-brother.'

'You're Mrs. Mortlock, are you, m'am?' said Mr. Budd. He eyed her sleepily, and came to the conclusion that whether it was a shock to her or not, she was thoroughly enjoying it. A good-looking woman, but with a hard mouth that was reflected in her eyes. 'I'd like you to tell us anything you can about the day preceding Lady Conyers tragic death.'

Mrs. Mortlock was only too willing. She burst into a flood of speech, describing in detail everything that had happened. But there was nothing that they had not already heard from Roger Marsden.

'Poor dear Sybil hadn't been very well, you know, for some time past,' she said. 'All those headaches she suffered from. I always said she ought to have done something about it. I'm afraid my step-brother was to blame for that. He never would take them seriously. It was his opinion that all she needed was more exercise and fresh air. But, of course, it was much more serious than he imagined. As this terrible affair has proved . . .'

'You think these headaches had somethin' to do with her death?' asked Mr. Budd as she paused for breath.

'Why, of course,' declared Mrs. Mortlock. 'They must have affected her mind, poor dear. That's why she did it.'

'It's your opinion that Lady Conyers took her own life?' inquired Mr. Budd gently.

Mrs. Mortlock nodded.

'I'm quite sure of it,' she said. 'I'm the only member of the household who thinks so, but I have no doubt whatever. She had been behaving *most* peculiarly for a long time. She would sit staring at nothing and never hear you if you spoke to her. I'm quite certain that her mind was slightly deranged.'

'How do you account for this bit out of a nursery rhyme that was scribbled on her bedroom door?' asked Mr. Budd.

Mrs. Mortlock shrugged the nursery rhyme out of existence.

'People who are not quite themselves sometimes do strange things,' she answered. 'Any other explanation is ridiculous. Nobody would want to poison Sybil — that's absurd. She *must* have done it herself.'

'Are you suggestin', m'am,' said Mr. Budd, 'that Lady Conyers' mind was so badly deranged that she suffered from homicidal tendencies?'

Mrs. Mortlock looked really shocked.

'Good gracious, no!' she exclaimed. 'What on earth put such an idea into your head?'

'It seems to me,' explained the stout

man, 'that that 'ud be the only way to account for your theory that the poor lady committed suicide.'

'I don't know what you mean,' she said.

Mr. Budd stifled a yawn.

'It couldn't be a coincidence,' he said, 'that there was another bit out of the same nursery rhyme on the door of Jackson's Folly, where that feller was killed. So the only conclusion you can come to is that, if as you think, Lady Conyers wrote the one on her door, she must've written the other. An' that implies that she was responsible for the death of Sam Sprigot . . . '

'That's impossible — impossible,' said Mrs. Mortlock, but there was no conviction in her voice.

'There's evidence that she was there that night,' said Mr. Budd. 'The scarf we found belonged to Lady Conyers . . . '

'But she didn't take it there,' broke in a voice from the door. '*I'll* tell you who took it there.'

They turned quickly.

Tony Harper was standing on the threshold.

7

He had come in so quietly that no one had heard him until he spoke. His face was strained, and Mr. Budd thought that he looked like someone who was near the point of physical exhaustion.

'Well now, sir,' said the stout superintendent smoothly, 'That's very interestin'. So you can tell us how Lady Conyers' scarf came to be found in Jackson's Folly, eh? Would you first mind tellin' us who you are?'

It was Mrs. Mortlock who supplied the information.

'This is Mr. Harper, my step-brother's secretary and estate manager,' she said, and the newcomer shot her a quick and rather resentful look. 'I can't imagine how you know anything about the scarf,' she continued. 'You've never mentioned it before . . . '

'No, sir,' broke in Inspector Crutchley. 'I questioned every one in the house about that scarf, including you, and you never said anything then.'

'Didn't I?' The tone of Harper's voice was a little defiant. 'Well, maybe I didn't . . . '

'Why was that?' said Mr. Budd in his most avuncular manner. 'You must've realised that it was important..?'

'I didn't want to make more trouble than there was already,' replied Harper. 'If you want to know who took that scarf, it was Sir Basil.'

'Basil!' exclaimed Mrs. Mortlock. 'What nonsense . . . '

'Oh no, it's not nonsense,' retorted Harper. 'He took it. I saw him.'

'I don't believe a word of it,' began Mrs. Mortlock angrily, but Mr. Budd stopped her.

'Just a minute, m'am, if you please,' he said. 'Let's get this straight. You saw Sir Basil Conyers take this scarf belonging to Lady Conyers, to Jackson's Folly?'

'I didn't see him actually take it to Jackson's Folly,' said Harper. 'But I saw him pick it up and put it in his pocket before he went out.'

Mrs. Mortlock uttered a sound that was suspiciously like a snort, but the big man ignored her.

'Tell us exactly what happened, sir,' he said.

'It was just after dinner,' explained Harper. 'Lady Conyers was carrying the scarf when she came down. She put it on the back of her chair when she sat down to dinner. When she left the table it was still on the back of her chair. Sir Basil picked it up and put it in the pocket of his dinner jacket . . . '

'I don't remember anything of the sort,' snapped Mrs. Mortlock.

'You'd already gone into the drawing-room,' said Harper. 'There was only Sir Basil and I left in the dining room.'

'I can't understand, sir,' said Inspector Crutchley, frowning. 'Why you couldn't have told us this before.'

'Neither can I,' declared Mrs. Mortlock. 'However, it's quite easily settled, isn't it? Sir Basil will be able to confirm it, if it's true.'

'If you think I'm lying . . . ' began Tony Harper, aggressively.

'We have to check these sort o' things, you know,' interrupted Mr. Budd diplomatically. 'Shortly after what you've been tellin' us, Sir Basil went out, didn't he?'

'Yes,' answered Harper sullenly. 'He forced himself on Angela . . . '

'Really,' said Mrs. Mortlock indignantly. 'I don't think it's necessary to go into all *that* . . . '

But Mr. Budd thought otherwise and said so. He insisted that Tony Harper should give a detailed account of what had happened, and Harper did so.

'It can have nothing to do with this other matter at all,' said Mrs. Mortlock disapprovingly. 'There was nothing in it. Just that my step-brother preferred to have company during his walk than to go alone. As a matter of fact he left Miss Trevor in the village . . . '

'Oh, he did, did he?' said Mr. Budd with interest. 'Now, where did he go?'

'I understand,' retorted Mrs. Mortlock, 'that he went to the Bull.'

'I see,' remarked the big man. 'What time did he come back?'

'I can't tell you,' she answered. 'I went

up to my room soon after he went out.'

Mr. Budd looked at Harper but he shook his head.

'I can't tell you, either,' he said. 'I never saw Sir Basil again that night. I had some work to do and I spent the rest of the evening doing it. I've a workroom near my bedroom.'

Inspector Crutchley cleared his throat.

'You heard somebody come in late, m'am, didn't you?' he interpolated. 'I remember you asking Miss Trevor and Sir Basil if it was either of them.'

She flushed, and there was an expression of annoyance on her face as she replied:

'I *did* think I heard someone about. But that was very late.'

'How late?' demanded Mr. Budd quickly.

'I don't know — it must have been after twelve. I had been in bed some time.'

'Is your room on the same floor as Lady Conyers?'

'Yes. It's at the other end of the corridor.'

'What was the sound you heard. Somebody moving about?'

'Yes. I thought I heard somebody come up the stairs . . . '

'And pass your door?'

She shook her head.

'No, they didn't pass my door. It was a very faint sound. I may have been mistaken.'

'Where's this workroom of yours, sir?' asked Mr. Budd, turning his sleepy eyes on Harper.

'On the floor above Mrs. Mortlock's,' said Harper. 'It wasn't me she heard, if that's what you mean. I never came down again.'

Mr. Budd asked several more questions but he failed to elicit anything further of interest. Neither was he more successful with Angela Trevor.

She had started off with Sir Basil but he had left her in the village. Almost immediately after he left her it had started to rain. She had taken shelter in the church porch until it had stopped for a while, and then gone back to Marbury Court. She didn't see anybody on her return and had gone straight up to her room.

They sought out the maid who had taken up the glass of water which Lady Conyers had every night. She was a buxom girl who had been in service at the Court since she had left school. She had taken up the water while everyone was at dinner. She had taken it early because, lately, Lady Conyers had been in the habit of going to bed early and she didn't like to be disturbed. The maid had heard nothing during the night. She slept with the other servants at the top of the other wing so it was unlikely that she would have.

Inspector Crutchley, who had been over all this ground before Mr. Budd's arrival in Marbury, was obviously bored. He was even more so when the stout man suggested that they should visit Lady Conyers' bedroom. However, he agreed with as good a grace as possible, and unlocked the door.

Mr. Budd stood on the threshold and looked round the dainty, beautifully furnished room with sleepy interest. The room had not been touched since the tragedy and, after a moment or two, he moved about slowly, peering at the various articles that lay scattered about just as Lady Conyers had left them.

Leek and Crutchley watched him from the doorway, the latter rather impatiently.

The glass of water and the sleeping tablets had been removed and tested for fingerprints, but there had been none with the exception of Lady Conyers' own.

'We searched the whole place thoroughly,' said Inspector Crutchley in answer to a murmured question from the big man. 'There was nothing to help us in this business.'

'It seems that if it *was* murder,' remarked Mr. Budd. 'It must have been an inside job. I don't see how anyone could've got in from outside very easily. Let's go an' see the gardener.'

This did surprise the inspector.

'Why do you want to see him?' he demanded.

'They've got some very nice roses here,' answered the stout superintendent. 'Very nice, indeed. Now, roses are a hobby o' mine. I've got some o' the best roses you ever saw at my little place at Streatham. Beautiful things.'

Inspector Crutchley was not in the least interested in roses. He said so.

'Ah,' said Mr. Budd, shaking his head sorrowfully. 'You've missed a lot in life if you don't like roses. One o' the loveliest flowers in the world, that's what they are.'

They found the gardener just on the point of going home to his cottage. They were lucky to have found him at all, as he explained at some length. If he hadn't been finishing putting in some cuttings in the greenhouse, they wouldn't have done.

Mr. Budd launched into admiration of the roses, and Leek and the inspector stood patiently by while they compared notes concerning pruning, budding, grafting, and the best fertilizer.

The conversation developed into a discussion on various kinds of garden pests.

'There's one thin',' remarked Mr. Budd, 'that I can't stand. Wasps. They scare me stiff. I expect you get a lot of 'em round here?'

The gardener admitted that they did get a good few. He pointed to an old tree trunk that sprawled picturesquely by a grass covered bank.

'Found a nest there t'other week,' he informed them. 'Dratted things. Got stung, I did.'

'There's a nest at Kenwiddy's,' said Mr. Budd unblushingly, and to Leek's surprise. 'Down at the bottom of the garden . . .'

'There's only one way ter take a wasps nest,' said the gardener. 'An' that's cyanide. Sulphur ain't no good, but cyanide finishes the beggers afore they know what's 'appened to 'em.'

Inspector Crutchley's expression changed. So this was why Mr. Budd had been so eager to talk to the gardener? His respect, which had been rapidly fading, took a turn in the opposite direction.

'I agree with you,' said Mr. Budd. 'I s'pose you couldn't let me have a bit? I'd like to take that nest.'

'You can 'ave some, an' welcome,' said the gardener. 'I've got a packet over in the shed.'

He led the way over to a toolshed, opened the door and went in. Going over to a shelf that stretched along one wall and was littered with all kinds of odd jars and bottles, he put up his hand to a spot near the other end.

And then he stopped, with his gnarled old fingers still crooked to take down the packed he had expected to find.

'Well now, that be queer,' he said wonderingly. 'It's gone. It was 'ere last week. I wonder who could a' took it?'

Mr. Budd wondered too. But he didn't have to wonder 'why'.

That was where the cyanide had come from that had killed Lady Conyers.

8

'Now we know where the cyanide came from,' remarked Mr. Budd as they left Marbury Court.

'Well, it would never have occurred to me to tackle the gardener,' declared Inspector Crutchley frankly. 'That was clever, that was.'

'You're not a gardener yourself, you see,' said the stout man. 'If you had been, you'd 've remembered how they take wasps nests.' He sighed. 'Well, we know where it came from, but we don't know who took it. That's not goin' to be so easy.'

'The whole thing's a puzzler,' said the inspector frowning. 'I don't know what to think. If it was one of the people back there,' he jerked his head in the direction of the Court, 'who poisoned 'er ladyship, it beats me which one it could've been.'

'Or the reason for it, eh?' added Mr. Budd. 'We've learned something fresh, anyhow. The cyanide an' that scarf.'

'We've got to confirm that with Sir Basil,' said Crutchley. 'I can't think why 'e didn't mention the fact that he'd picked it up when I was telling him about it the other morning.'

'That's certainly interestin' an' peculiar,' said Mr. Budd thoughtfully. 'Pity we didn't see him. I wonder where he got to?'

'Gone for a walk somewhere,' answered the inspector. ''E's a wonderful man for exercise.'

'Like my Sergeant,' said Mr. Budd, looking at the silent Leek. 'Only he takes all his lyin' down.'

'I don't believe in exercise fer exercise sake,' said Leek shaking his thin head. 'It's 'ere — ' he tapped his forehead ' — that the work gets done.'

'You must've been on strike for a long time!' grunted Mr. Budd. 'If you're not in a hurry to get back, Inspector,' he added. 'I'd like to have a look at this place, Jackson's Folly.'

The inspector was not in a hurry, and they turned off in the direction of the ruined house. Mr. Budd, himself, was not a great lover of physical exercise. He boasted that he never walked if he could ride, and never rode if he could remain where he was. It wasn't very far to Jackson's Folly, but it was quite far enough for the stout man. Luckily, it was all down hill.

In the lane that led down to the hollow in which the house was sited, they met a middle-aged woman coming towards them. She was thin and rather angular, and her rather large nose was very slightly blue at the tip. She was walking fast and breathing a little heavily. Neither Mr. Budd, nor either of the others with him, had ever met Miss Titmarsh or they would have recognised her.

She passed them quickly with only the merest sidelong glance, but Mr. Budd, whose sleepy eyes missed nothing, thought he detected an expression of dismay mingled with fear in that glance, and wondered what had induced it.

It was a quiet, still evening. The sun was low down in the west, casting long shadows over the rank grass from tree and hedge. They turned in at the broken gate and came into the dusky twilight of the weed-covered drive.

'Gloomy sort o' spot,' remarked the big man. 'Ideal for a meetin' place, if you wanted to keep your meetin' private.'

It was Leek who first caught sight of the paper on the partly open door and drew their attention to it. But Mr. Budd had seen it at almost the same moment and so had Inspector Crutchley.

It was a page torn from an exercise book and on it, in blue pencil, had been printed: 'THIS IS THE DOG THAT WORRIED THE CAT'.

Mr. Budd uttered an exclamation.

'I don't like the look o' this,' he said. 'I don't like the look of it at all . . . '

He squeezed his large body through the narrow gap of the partly open door and found himself in the almost dark hall. There was a squeaking scurry as he moved cautiously forward, peering into the semi-darkness. Presently, as his eyes became accustomed to the gloom, he was able to dimly distinguish the bulk of the big staircase, and the jutting whitish-blur of the fireplace.

And he saw something else — something that lay in front of that fireplace forming a darker, more substantial, shadow among the other shadows . . .

By this time he had been joined by Leek and Inspector Crutchley.

'Good God Almighty,' muttered the inspector, 'not — *another* . . . '

'I'm afraid so,' answered Mr. Budd.

He picked his way through the dust and debris to that vague shape that sprawled as still and silent as the stillness and silence that surrounded it.

He bent down, pulled out a box of matches, and struck one.

As the match flared into flame, Inspector Crutchley gave a sharp exclamation.

'It's Sir Basil Conyers!' he said. 'Is he dead?'

'Nobody could live after *that*,' answered Mr. Budd and pointed to the crushed-in head.

'Just like Sprigot,' said Crutchley, under his breath.

Mr. Budd nodded and dropped the

match which was burning his fingers.

'I don't think there's much doubt that the same person killed 'em both,' he said. 'There's a very busy killer at work in this neighbourhood — a very busy killer, indeed.'

⋆ ⋆ ⋆

Mr. Budd lay on the bed in his lavender-scented room in Kenwiddy's farm and stared at the ceiling. Between his teeth was the remains of one of his black cigars but it had long since gone out.

Outside it was quite dark for the hour was late, and the rest of the household, including the lugubrious Sergeant Leek, had gone to bed. Mr. Budd, however, although he lay on his bed, was still fully dressed.

Following the discovery of the dead body of Sir Basil Conyers in Jackson's Folly there had been a great deal of feverish activity as the usual routine procedure in the case of murder was put into operation.

The police station at Greystock had been notified at once and photographers and fingerprint men had arrived in a police car, accompanied by a surprised Superintendent Sones and the police surgeon. The people at Marbury Court had been told of the tragedy and, eventually the body of Sir Basil had been removed for the post mortem examination.

It was not until all this had been done, and he had had a long talk with Sones, that Mr. Budd, weary after a fairly busy day, was able to get back to the farm for a rest. He foresaw a long and strenuous day before him on the morrow and after a pot of tea — the Kenwiddys had wanted to lay a cold supper, but the gargantuan tea which he had eaten on his arrival had proved sufficient to last him until breakfast and he had declined — he had gone straight up to his room.

Physically weary, he had lain down for what he intended should be a moment, and had become so enrapt in his thoughts that he had forgotten the passing of time. His brain was as alert as it usually was, and he was putting into practice one of his invariable methods when tackling a new case. He was going through the whole thing, as far as he knew it, point by point, sorting out the pieces as he might have sorted the various pieces of a jig-saw puzzle before trying to put the picture together.

The starting point was Sam Sprigot. The little larcenist had come out of prison after serving a sentence for his last robbery and taken a room with Mrs. Bagley. But he hadn't done that at once. There was an interval of three months from the time he left the prison to the time he turned up at Mrs. Bagley's lodging house. What had happened to him during that period? Where had he been and, equally important, what had he been doing? Had something happened to him during this three months that had culminated in his murder at Jackson's Folly? This seemed likely. But *what* had happened?

It was impossible to conjecture. It might have been anything. Even after he had come to Mrs. Bagley's his behaviour had been peculiar. He had remained in his room during the day and only gone out at night. What had he done during these nocturnal excursions? Again it was impossible to conjecture. Only Sam Sprigot could say that and he was dead.

It was fairly safe to conclude that it was the letter he had received in the morning that had brought him down to Marbury. Who had written that letter? And for what reason had the meeting, if meeting it was, been arranged at Jackson's Folly?

Concerning this, Mr. Budd thought that it might be worth trying to follow up the vague idea which had occurred to him when he had been thinking over the nursery rhyme. He repeated the beginning of it to himself.

'*This is the house that Jack built.*
This is the malt which lay in the
   house that Jack built.'

That was it. The malt! Was there something valuable in Jackson's Folly, or had there been something valuable there, that Sam Sprigot knew about? Was that the reason why the murderer had killed him and scrawled that bit of the rhyme on a sheet of paper and pinned it to the door: '*This is the rat that ate the malt that lay in the house that Jack built*'?

If there *had* been something hidden there which Sam knew about and, perhaps, during that unaccounted three months, removed, there was reason for that bit of rhyme. But if something like this was the explanation, how did Lady Conyers come into it? And not only she but her husband as well. That was something that Mr. Budd, try as he would, couldn't fathom out.

As he lay staring up at the ceiling of his room, he racked his brains to form some reasonable theory that would link these people with Sam Sprigot, and he racked them in vain.

He gave up that angle at length and concentrated on what, if anything, there could have been hidden in the ruined house that was so valuable. The proceeds of some robbery? That might be it and that would tie up with Sam Sprigot. Maybe, Sam had heard about it while he was in prison — such things had happened — and decided to pinch it at the first opportunity. But the first opportunity would have been, surely, immediately after he came out of prison? He wouldn't have waited for more than three months. Unless, this was a possibility, he was waiting for someone else to come out of prison too? That would account for the letter. But in that case, why should the letter have given him such a scare?

Sam had never pulled off anything very big during his nefarious career, so it was hardly likely that if there was anything of value in Jackson's Folly it was the result of his own depredations.

However, it was worth following up. Mr. Budd made a mental note to get on to the Yard and ask for a dossier of the little crook's activities. It might lead to something or it might not. At the present juncture, he couldn't afford to neglect anything.

Three murders and practically no clues. It wasn't a very bright outlook.

There was the woman they had met on

their way to the ruined house. Was she mixed up in it? It seemed hardly likely, but the stout man remembered that momentary look he had seen in her eyes as she had passed them, and wondered. He had discovered who she was, the village school mistress . . . And the bit out of the nursery rhyme pinned on the door had been written on a page torn out of an exercise book. It had been written, too, in blue pencil . . .

Mr. Budd's recollections of his own schooldays associated a blue pencil with marked lessons. But lots of other people beside schoolteachers used blue pencils, and exercise books were common.

It would be worth having a word with the woman, though. What was her name? Titmarsh, that was it. He'd do that in the morning. After the inquest.

He got heavily off the bed and slowly undressed. He was tired and depressed. For he couldn't see his way clearly. He had no plan to follow. He would just have to wait, hopefully, that something would turn up to give him a lead . . .

He got into bed, but it was some time

before he fell asleep, and then it was fitful and broken.

Deep down in his subconscious mind something was struggling to force its way up, but it wasn't until several days later that it succeeded . . .

★　★　★

Miss Titmarsh did not sleep at all that night. She lay staring into the darkness, conscious of every faint sound that broke the silence of her little cottage.

What should she do? What *could* she do? Over and over again the question circled her brain, never stopping and never answered.

At last she could stand it no longer and getting up, put on her dressing-gown and went into her neat kitchen to make herself a cup of tea.

It was nearly four o'clock as she sat at the small table and sipped the tea. She would have to get some sleep, or she would never get through the coming day. The thought of the schoolroom and all the children was a nightmare. How *could* she concentrate on her work when at any moment disaster might overtake her?

She poured herself out another cup of tea and took three aspirin tablets. Perhaps they would sooth her jangled nerves . . .

After a little while, she went back to bed and tried to settle down to sleep. But it was no use. When the sun began to filter round the drawn curtains, she was still lying, wide awake, her mind fearful and beset with the problem to which she could find no solution.

9

The inquest on Sam Sprigot had been scheduled for ten o'clock in the church hall, and by half-past nine most of the inhabitants of Marbury had congregated outside the small building in the hope of getting a free and sensational entertainment.

With the advent of television, sensation in every conceivable form was not unknown to the people of Marbury, but this was different, this was not confined to a small screen, this was real and their very own.

Major Panting was talking to the Reverend Oswald Hornbeam when Mr. Budd arrived in company with Inspector Crutchley and the melancholy Sergeant Leek.

'You seem to have been right, Rector,' remarked the major, as the big man came within hearing. 'It certainly looks as though something evil *had* been loosed in the village, by jove! Three violent deaths within less than a week.'

The rector shook his head sadly, and his troubled face was grave.

'This latest murder,' he said, 'Poor Sir Basil Conyers — is quite incredible — quite incredible.'

'Meanin' that you find the other two deaths credible, sir?' asked Mr. Budd sleepily, as he joined them.

'No, no,' the rector looked a little shocked. 'Of course, that was not my meaning. But it seems incredible . . . first that unfortunate man, then Lady Conyers, and now Sir Basil . . .'

'It is incredible,' agreed Mr. Budd. 'An' that means that it's incredible to us because we don't know the beginnin' of it. I'll bet it's quite simple when you know the 'how' an' the 'why'. Like most things.'

'Biggest sensation we've ever had here,' said Major Panting. 'Made more of a rumpus in the village than that spy business during the war. Jackson's Folly was mixed up with that, too.'

Mr. Budd pricked up his ears.

'What was that, sir?' he asked.

Major Panting was only too willing to recount the incident. It was one of the highlights of his life. Although he was known in the village of Marbury as 'Major' the only legitimate claim he had for the title was because he had been the Officer Commanding Marbury's Home Guard. To give him his due, the Home Guard had come into existence entirely through his own efforts. He had been indefatigable in enlisting recruits, had drilled them, insisted on regular rifle practice and exercises, and had certainly, with the material he had, turned out a fairly smart body of men. They turned out regularly for duty, patrolling the countryside from darkness until dawn, vigilantly watchful for any untoward happening that be construed as 'enemy action'.

It was during one of these nightly reconnaissances that one of the men found a small torn portion of silk that had, quite obviously, formed part of a parachute. The man had taken it to Major Panting, and the major at once jumped to the conclusion, rightly as it turned out, that the Germans had dropped a spy by parachute and that he had landed in or near Marbury. His reasons for this conclusion were not without a certain amount of foundation.

There were no troops stationed in the neighbourhood and there had been no air raid on Marbury, or within a radius of twenty miles, for a considerable period. The portion of silk which had been found had not been exposed to the weather for very long, so it could hardly have had anything to do with a raid.

With great energy and excitement, Major Panting ordered a thorough search of the district, and to the surprise of the majority, if not his own, a man was discovered hiding in Jackson's Folly. There was no doubt that he was a spy or that he had landed by a parachute from an enemy plane. He was provided with false papers, English money, and all the necessary equipment to sustain life until he could reach his 'contact'. Unfortunately for him, he had injured his leg in landing and had been forced to hide-up in the ruined house until it was well enough for him to walk.

The man was handed over to the authorities and questioned, but steadfastly refused to talk, so that it was never discovered who the 'contact' was to whom he would have reported. Major Panting received a letter of congratulations and thanks from the powers that be, and that was the end of the incident.

Mr. Budd listened to this story with interest. There seemed to be no possible connection between it and the present case, but he filed it away in the capacious storehouse of his memory with all the other odds and ends that reposed there, ready to be brought out and examined should the occasion arise.

By this time the coroner, a small, finicky man with quite the largest horn-rimmed spectacles that Mr. Budd had ever seen, and which gave him rather the appearance of a baby owl, had arrived, and the waiting crowd were pouring into the church hall.

If they had come with the expectation of excitement they were soon disappointed.

As soon as the jury had been sworn, the coroner opened the proceedings by a brief speech explaining what they were there for, which everybody knew without his telling them, gave a short lecture on the legal limitations of an inquest, and called for evidence of identification of the deceased. This was supplied by Inspector Crutchley and came as a surprise to the majority of the people present. The Reverend Oswald Hornbeam was the next witness and he described how he had come to find the body. He was followed by the police surgeon who gave evidence concerning the cause of death. At the conclusion of his evidence, Inspector Crutchley asked for an adjournment.

This was granted, obviously rather grudgingly, by the coroner, and the inquest on Lady Conyers was opened. This was even shorter and less sensational than the inquest on Sam Sprigot.

Only evidence of identification, and the medical evidence as to the cause of death, were taken and then, once again, Inspector Crutchley got up and said his piece and the inquiry was, again reluctantly on the part of the coroner, adjourned.

The crowd that had swarmed into the church hall swarmed out again feeling, if the odd murmurs and scraps of conversation were anything to go by, cheated of their expected enjoyment.

An elderly, grey-haired man, who had come in with the people from Marbury Court, came over to Mr. Budd and introduced himself as the family solicitor. His name was Titer, of Holdfast, Titer and Titer, a firm of solicitors in Greystock who had looked after the legal side of the estate for over a century.

'This is a very terrible business,' he said in a dry, rather crackling voice, as though his staple diet might have consisted of withered parchment. 'A terrible and inexplicable business. I trust that it will soon be cleared up and the — er — person or persons responsible brought to justice.'

Mr. Budd concurred with this heartily.

'I can only conclude,' went on Mr. Titer, clearing his throat without making any appreciable difference in the dry, rasping quality of his voice, 'that we have to deal with a lunatic. There can, so far as I can see, be nothing to connect this man, Sprigot, with my — er — clients.'

Mr. Budd, being in precisely the same state of mind himself, admitted that 'there didn't appear to be any connection at present'. He concluded by asking a question.

'Who inherits the estate?'

Mr. Titer, with that curious reluctance on the part of all lawyers to give a straightforward answer to a straightforward question, coughed and looked down his rather long thin nose.

'That is a matter which will have to be gone into, of course,' he answered slowly. 'Yes, it will have to be gone into. Sir Basil and Lady Conyers died without issue. The house and the lands are entailed. The — er — money they were entitled to leave to whom they pleased, but it was always accepted that it should go with the — er — rest . . . '

'Does it in this case?' asked Mr. Budd.

'Sir Basil left a will leaving everything to his wife,' said Mr. Titer, 'but, of course, since she predeceased him, that becomes invalid. H'm. Yes, invalid. So far as I know, Lady Conyers died intestate.'

Mr. Budd curbed his not unnatural impatience.

'Which means that everything goes to the next of kin, doesn't it?' he said.

Mr. Titer pursed his thin lips and, after a pause, admitted that that was so.

'Who is the next of kin?' inquired the stout man, feeling that getting information out of Mr. Titer was a lengthy and difficult procedure.

'We shall have to go into that,' replied the lawyer. 'Sir Basil has, or had, a younger brother, who would, if he is still alive, be the natural heir . . . '

'Don't you *know* whether he's alive or not?' demanded Mr. Budd.

'Nothing has been seen or heard of him for over twenty years,' said Mr. Titer. 'Dear me, yes, it must be slightly longer than that. He was — er — the black sheep of the family, I'm afraid. Always in trouble of one sort or another — mostly money. Eventually, he forged a cheque for a very considerable sum and disappeared. He hasn't been heard of from that day to this. But, if he is still alive, as I say, he would be the heir.'

'An' if he's dead?' said Mr. Budd.

'In that case,' said Mr. Titer, 'provided he had no children, Mrs. Mortlock would seem to be the next of kin.'

Mr. Budd frowned. This was something new. It might not have any connection with the present case but it was something to remember and take into consideration.

'What is the name of this younger brother?' he asked.

'Francis Conyers,' said Mr. Titer. 'That is, or perhaps was, his name.'

'What is the value of the estate?' said Mr. Budd. 'I understand that Sir Basil was rather fond of racin' an' that he'd lost a great deal of money at it.'

Mr. Titer's lips compressed. This, from his expression, was a subject that was distasteful to him.

'Sir Basil,' he remarked at length, 'was very foolish in many respects. He lost a — er — considerable sum in gambling on the turf. In fact most of his own fortune. But Lady Conyers was a very wealthy woman. I cannot, of course, give you the exact amount of the estate but it is very considerable — in the region of four to five hundred thousand pounds.'

Mr. Budd screwed up his lips in a silent whistle. He had had no idea that such an enormous sum was involved. Here was motive and to spare for murder. If Francis Conyers was still alive, and there was nothing to show that he wasn't, he would have every reason for wishing the deaths of his brother and his wife. But none whatever for Sam Sprigot. There was the snag. How did he come into it? Perhaps he had known Francis Conyers? But even if he had what reason was there for his death? And then there was Mrs. Mortlock. If Francis Conyers wasn't alive and hadn't left any children, then Mrs. Mortlock was the heiress to a fortune . . .

Mr. Budd sighed. He had learned quite a lot more about the case, but what he had learned only served to make it more complicated. He took his leave of Mr. Titer and, accompanied by the melancholy Leek, went in search of Miss Titmarsh.

An inquiry the previous night had elicited the fact that she was the village schoolmistress from Mrs. Kenwiddy, who had recognized her from Mr. Budd's description.

The children were just coming out for lunch when he reached the school-house, and he caught Miss Titmarsh as she was following with the same object.

Her thin face went paler as she saw Mr. Budd and again he saw the flicker of fear in her eyes.

'Well, really,' she said a little breathlessly, 'I don't know *how* I can help you . . . '

'I was wonderin' if you saw anyone in the neighbourhood of Jackson's Folly yesterday evenin'?' said Mr. Budd. 'You was comin' from that direction when you passed us in the lane.'

Miss Titmarsh leaned against her desk. Her lips seemed to have suddenly gone dry for she moistened them quickly with the tip of her tongue.

'No — no, I'm afraid I saw no one,' she answered. 'I — I only passed the gate, you know — on my way back from my little walk.'

'You didn't see Sir Basil?' asked the stout man and she shook her head.

'I saw no one, no one at all,' she declared. 'What a very shocking affair. Dear me, I really don't know what is happening round here. It used to be so peaceful . . . '

Her hands were shaking as she fumbled with her worn bag.

'It's a nasty business,' said Mr. Budd, 'but I hope it won't be long before we get to the bottom of it.'

'Have — have the police got a clue to — to the murderer?' she asked quickly.

'We've several lines we're followin' up,' said Mr. Budd evasively. 'I suppose you've never heard of a feller called Sprigot — Sam Sprigot?'

'No, indeed,' answered Miss Titmarsh. 'How should I be likely to know anything about a man like that?'

'Like what, miss?' murmured the stout man gently.

'A burglar,' said Miss Titmarsh. 'I should be hardly likely to come in contact with that sort of person.'

'No, I suppose you wouldn't,' agreed

Mr. Budd and yawned.

He asked one or two more questions and then, as Miss Titmarsh showed signs of restiveness, he took his departure.

'How did she know?' he remarked, as he and the lean sergeant made their way down the High Street in the direction of Kenwiddy's farm.

'How did she know what?' demanded Leek.

'That Sprigot was a burglar?' said his superior thoughtfully. 'Nobody knew round here, not even his name, until this mornin' at the inquest, an' she wasn't there . . .'

'P'raps somebody told 'er,' suggested Leek.

Mr. Budd shook his head.

'I should doubt it,' he said. 'There wouldn't have been time. An' yet she knew . . . H'm — interestin' an' peculiar!'

10

The inquest on Sir Basil Conyers, which took place two days after the inquest on his wife and Sam Sprigot, was as speedy and unproductive of excitement as the previous ones. Once more the police asked for, and obtained, an adjournment although the coroner couldn't resist adding a comment to the effect that he hoped they would soon be able to produce evidence that would lead to an arrest.

The general opinion in the village was that there was a lunatic at large and in consequence few people ventured out after nightfall.

All the children were warned, to their great annoyance and irritation, that Jackson's Folly must be avoided even in the daytime, and Miss Titmarsh put up a notice to this effect in the schoolroom.

Mr. Budd, during the days that followed, was a greatly worried man. He could find nothing at all to give him even the faintest lead. The result was that he grew more and more irritable and the unfortunate Sergeant Leek had to bear the brunt of his superior's feeling of frustration.

Everything that it was possible to follow-up, the stout superintendent had followed-up. Sam Sprigot's dossier had been sent down from Scotland Yard, and Mr. Budd had gone carefully through it, but he could find nothing to help him.

The little man's record was mostly one of petty crime and the biggest haul he had ever made was jewellery valued at under two thousand pounds from a flat off Maida Vale. The robbery for which he had served his last stretch had, apparently, netted him nothing at all, for he had made a mistake in the flat he had entered, by climbing the stackpipe to the balcony, and broken into the one next to it, instead. Obviously the flat he had intended was Miss Ursula Westland's, the actress, but his mistake had landed him in the empty flat of a gentleman called Danesford, a bachelor, who was away.

There was nothing of value here, although Sam had obviously made a pretty thorough search, and his luck was completely out, for, climbing back down the pipe, he had fallen into the arms of a waiting policeman, who had recognized him instantly and carted him off to the police station.

The search for the whereabouts of Francis Conyers had begun, but so far there was no news of him. It was rather like looking for a needle in a haystack. The man, if he were still alive, might be anywhere.

An advertisement in the newspapers stating that if he applied to Messrs: Holdfast, Titer and Titer, he would 'hear of something to his advantage' had brought no result. The whole case had come to a complete standstill. Someone had killed Sam Sprigot; someone had killed Lady Conyers and Sir Basil, but who they were was a mystery. Mrs. Mortlock, if she was aware that Francis Conyers was no longer alive, might be looked upon as a suspect with an excellent motive so far as Lady Conyers and her husband's death was concerned, but there was no motive, or anything else, to link her with the death of Sam Sprigot. Nor could Mr. Budd, although he racked his brains until his head ached, discover any reason for the recurring nursery rhyme that ran as a *liet motif* through the whole affair.

'Why should anyone write that bit out o' the House that Jack Built an' leave it on the door?' he asked Leek, not for the first time, but the lean sergeant could only shake his head. 'It's gettin' me down, that's what it's doin',' declared Mr. Budd. 'I've never come across a case where there was so little to go on.'

'Maybe somethin' 'ull pop up,' said Leek hopefully.

'Maybe,' snarled Mr. Budd sarcastically. 'P'raps Sam's ghost 'ull come an' tell us who killed him, or p'raps you'll think of something sensible — they're both equally unlikely.'

'You don't suppose that this feller what was dropped by parachute durin' the war's got anythin' ter do with it, do yer?' asked Leek.

'I've thought o' that,' answered his

superior, 'but I can't see how he can.'

'I read in a book once,' said Leek, 'about one of these fellers the Germans dropped over 'ere to spy. He was given lots an' lots of money ter bring with 'im. Maybe this feller 'ad a lot o' money on him an' hid it in that old 'ouse.'

'An' after all this time these people suddenly have an inspiration that it's there, eh?' grunted Mr. Budd.

'They could've found out,' said Leek.

'Can you imagine Sir Basil an' Lady Conyers goin' after a bunch of money that a German spy had hidden in the place?' demanded Mr. Budd crossly. 'Because if you can, I can't.'

'You never can tell what people 'ull do,' said the lean sergeant truthfully. 'They don't always do what you'd expect.'

'The only person who does what you'd expect is you — an' that's nothin',' snapped the stout man. 'If this spy feller had hidden any money in Jackson's Folly, how did Sam Sprigot get to hear of it? I suppose you're goin' to tell me that somebody told him an' then killed him when he went after it, an' that he an' the

Conyers' was all in it together?'

Leek sighed.

'I was only makin' a suggestion,' he said. 'Tryin' to be a bit helpful . . . '

Mr. Budd's annoyance evaporated. Perhaps he had been a bit irritable. They were sitting in the garden at the farm, and he hoisted himself out of his chair.

'I don't think there's much use followin' that line,' he said in a more conciliatory manner. 'The thing that worries me is linkin' all these people together. Whoever killed 'em, killed 'em all for the same reason. If you can think of somethin' that 'ud be common to all three of 'em we might be gettin' somewhere.'

But the melancholy sergeant's ideas were exhausted and he could only shake his head mournfully.

'The thing I'd like to know,' continued Mr. Budd, 'is what happened to Sprigot durin' the time 'e left prison an' the time he turned up at Mrs. Bagley's lodgings. Where was he an' what was he doin'? If we knew that, we'd be a good bit nearer to findin' out the truth.'

He thrust a fat finger and thumb into his waistcoat pocket and drew out one of his black cigars. After frowning at it gloomily for a moment, he stuck it between his teeth and lit it.

'I'm goin' to my room to have a good think,' he said. 'If you get any bright ideas — and I mean bright an' not a lot o' tomfoolery like you generally get into your head — you can let me know.'

He lumbered off and disappeared into the house.

Leek, with another sigh, watched him go and then opened the exercise book on his knee and began laboriously to write. But his mind was not on his autobiography, and, after a little while, he closed the book again and stuck the pencil he had been using into his pocket.

Although Mr. Budd had scoffed at his idea that there was something hidden in the old house, Leek was still convinced that he was right. Deep down in his subconscious mind was an enormous belief in his own capabilities. One of his favourite occupations was indulging in fantastic daydreams wherein he performed the most remarkable and amazing feats with effort-less ease. He was quite convinced that, given the opportunity, all these achieve-ments could be as readily transformed into the realm of fact.

Actually, and unsuspected by most people, Leek was a supreme egotist and it was this trait in his character that enabled him to put up with Mr. Budd's irritability and sometimes caustic humour, and to treat it with a kind of resigned tolerance. It was just a way that his superior had of expressing himself and was not to be taken seriously. It was a little trying at times, but the best way was to ignore it.

Leek was supremely satisfied with himself and couldn't see why anyone else should be dissatisfied. Therefore, the fact that Mr. Budd had refused to take his suggestion seriously did not effect Leek's opinion of it in the least. It was a good one. As he sat staring at the sunlit garden, he went over it again in his mind, and the more he thought of it, the more convinced he became that he was right. But, of course, Mr. Budd wouldn't do anything about it. If it had been his *own* idea, it would have been a different matter . . .

And then a brilliant thought suddenly occurred to him.

Supposing he could prove that he was right? That would be a feather in his cap. Old Budd would have to climb down and apologise then, wouldn't he? For a minute or two he sat lost in contemplation of the imaginative picture that this conjured up. He would do it!

He got up, went into the house and put away his exercise book and pencil, and, arming himself with a large electric torch from his bag, came quietly out again and set off down the lane.

If he could bring the case which was baffling Budd to a successful conclusion, solve the mystery entirely on his own, what a triumph that would be. He could see, in his mind's eye, the complete stupefaction of the stout superintendent when he announced that he had discovered the truth. And not only that, but it would probably lead to his promotion. Detective Inspector Leek!

With his mind full of rosy imaginings,

he hurried along through the scented countryside, his long, thin legs moving faster than they had moved for a considerable time.

The sun was sinking in the west and there were long shadows stretching across field and meadow to herald the approach of night. The lane leading down to Jackson's Folly looked gloomy and uninviting in the twilight — a narrow tunnel edged with straggling hedges and roofed by the interlacing of the branches overhead.

It was very silent and still. Only the faint rustle as some small animal moved in the undergrowth, and the twittering of the birds in the trees, broke the silence.

Leek came at last to the broken gate leading to Jackson's Folly. He paused for a moment looking about him, but there was no sign of human life. The lane behind him stretched away in a deserted funnel of leafy green, and the weed-grown drive in front of him was dark and forbidding. He could smell the dankness of rotting vegetation and gnats brushed his face.

A little more slowly now, he walked up

the drive and came to the porch with its broken door. It had been barricaded up since the murder of Sir Basil and there was now no way in that way, but undeterred, Leek made his way round the house until he came to a broken window at the back. Through this he climbed carefully and found himself in what had once been the kitchen. It was now a wreckage of fallen brick and plaster. The ceiling had broken away in two places, leaving great blackened gaps of protruding laths. A rusty range filled the big fireplace, and a huge sink, full of rubbish, stood under a narrow window from which all the glass had long since vanished.

Leek brushed the cobwebs from his hair and face and took out his torch, for it was almost dark inside. Switching it on, he moved the light from side to side revealing some broken china and a heap of old pots and saucepans.

He had been so full of his dreams of triumph that the magnitude of his task had not come fully home to him, but now, as he stood in the ruin of the old kitchen, he realised just what difficulties lay ahead.

Somewhere in this rotting shell of a house lay hidden, if he was right and it never occurred to him for a moment that he wasn't, a large sum of money, concealed there by the man who had been sent to act as a spy. Somewhere..?

That was the difficulty. Where? The house was a large one. The hiding place could be anywhere . . .

Leek decided that he might as well start with the ground floor and began to make a systematic search of the kitchen. He went over every inch of it meticulously, turning over the rubbish, examining the floor and the walls, and found — nothing.

The door to the passage had long since been reduced to a heap of rotting timber and he moved through the opening into the short, narrow passage that led to the great hall. He was careful to search this passage with the same care that he had expended on the kitchen and with the same result.

It was unlikely, he though, that the spy had used the upstairs rooms at all. His leg had been injured in landing, injured badly enough to force him to seek refuge in the ruined house, so it was doubtful if he would have been able to negotiate the stairs. The most likely place, therefore, for him to choose to hide anything would be the ground floor.

Well, there was still plenty of that to explore. The great hall, and the two big rooms that opened off it.

Leek came to the archway that opened into the hall, and hesitated. It was nearly quite dark outside, now, and it would take him a long time to complete his search. Perhaps it would be better to give it up for that night and start again in the morning. But in the morning there might not be a chance. Budd might send him off on some job or other and there would be no opportunity. Better get on with it while the going was good.

He had decided to start with the room on the right, and had just begun to pick his way across the hall, when he heard a sound that brought him to a dead stop.

With straining ears, he stood motionless, listening.

Silence!

He came to the conclusion that what he had heard was the movement of a rat or some other creature, and he was just on the point of continuing his way, when he heard the sound again!

There was no mistaking it this time. It was a loud creak and it came from the direction of the room he was making for.

With his nerves strung up like taut wires, he stopped again, trying to locate the sound above the sudden thumping of his heart. For a moment he could hear nothing and then, quite loudly, there came a thud followed by the sound of a soft footstep crossing a wooden floor.

Somebody had entered the old house . . .

11

Leek stepped noiselessly backwards and crouched down in the shadow of the big staircase.

There was definitely someone in that room — someone who had entered by way of the window. He could hear them moving about uncertainly.

A tinge of colour crept into his pale cheeks and he felt his pulses throbbing with excitement. Was he on the verge of making an important discovery? Suppose this was the murderer . . . ?

He waited almost holding his breath, but now there was no sound from the room across the hall. The person in there, whoever-it-was, had stopped, probably to listen too. Leek could almost see him standing there, leaning slightly forward, alert and watchful.

And then he heard him again, a stealthy movement as he came nearer to the door. It hung half off its hinges, leaving a gap round the edge through which it was possible to squeeze. It was very dark but there was just enough light left to distinguish this gap as a darker shadow in the shadows that surrounded it. Leek, his eyes strained to their utmost, stared at the gap, and his hand gripped tighter on the torch.

There was a long interval and then, dimly, he made out a faint whitish blob, where the face of a person would be, floating in the shadowy gap. There was a suppressed grunt and the unknown visitor was out in the hall. Leek could see him standing there, motionless. He could hear his rather laboured breathing.

The lean sergeant debated with himself what he should do. Should he switch on the torch and see who it was, or should he wait and try and find out what the other was going to do?

He decided to wait. Perhaps this unknown newcomer would lead him to what he had been looking for . . .

The shadowy figure by the door stirred. It began to move slowly and cautiously forward. Dimly, Leek could see that it was peering from side to side with quick, jerky little movements of the head as though it was nervous. It moved stealthily to the centre of the hall and then towards the arch that led to the passage and the kitchen. Here it stopped again and listened.

Leek leaned forward to peer round the foot of the staircase and, in doing so, his torch came in contact with the wood-work. The sound was slight but it was sufficient. The listening figure started, and swung round with an exclamation. Leek, realising that further concealment was useless, and determined to discover who the unknown was, pressed the button on his torch and directed a blinding ray of light on the face of the figure by the archway.

It was the Reverend Oswald Hornbeam!

Leek gave a startled shout and scrambled to his feet.

'Here,' he said, 'What are you doing sneakin' about this place?'

'Who are you?' demanded the rector in a voice that held a faint quaver in its tone. 'Who are you?'

'I'm Detective-Sergeant Leek,' answered the lean man sternly, 'I'd like to know what you're doing here, sir?'

The Reverend Oswald Hornbeam uttered a gasp of relief. He drew a handkerchief from his pocket and wiped his face.

'Dear me,' he said huskily, 'that was really one of the most terrifying moments of my life . . . I must admit that I thought you were the murderer.'

'I thought you were,' said Leek. 'What are you doin' 'ere, sir, at this time of the evenin'?'

'I was passing along the road at the back,' answered the Reverend Oswald Hornbeam, 'I had been visiting one of my parishioners who is sick. I saw a light in the back portion of this house and I decided to investigate. Of course, I'd no idea it was a member of the police . . . ' He wiped his face again and put the handkerchief back in his pocket. 'You are — you are looking for clues, I presume?'

Leek explained the reason he was there and the rector listened with interest.

'Dear me,' he said, 'it would never have occurred to me that there might be anything of value hidden here.' He looked vaguely round the dark hall. 'I should doubt very much indeed if such a thing could be true. At the time that the — er — man was discovered hiding here a very extensive search was made — very extensive indeed. I hardly imagine that anything would have been overlooked. Of course, one can never tell. It's possible, but I hardly think likely.' He shook his head. 'However, as I said, one never can tell.'

Leek's faith in his own idea remained unshaken. He was convinced that there was something hidden in that old house — something of sufficient value to account for the murders, but it was evident that his search, for that night at least, would have to be cancelled.

The rector was obviously ill-at-ease and anxious to be gone. It must, the sergeant thought, have taken a great deal of courage on the Reverend Oswald's part to have come, alone, to investigate the light he had seen, after what had happened in that old house. But he was trembling a little now that the reaction had set in.

He welcomed Leek's suggestion that they should go, and followed the lean sergeant back through the kitchen to the window by which he had made his entrance. Leek went first and assisted the Reverend Oswald Hornbeam to climb out the small window. It had been easy for Leek to negotiate, but the more bulky form of the rector got wedged half-way.

'I'm afraid, I'm stuck,' he gasped, as he vainly tried to force himself through the narrow window.

Leek grasped him by the shoulders and pulled. The rotten woodwork of the window gave way, and the rector with part of the frame draped round his shoulders, shot through the opening like a cork from a bottle, and landed in a heap at the lean sergeant's feet. At the same moment there was a rumbling crash as the brickwork above the window, denuded of the support which the wooden frame-work had supplied, broke away and fell in a shower of dust and old mortar.

The Reverend Oswald Hornbeam scrambled to his feet and surveyed the wreckage in mild dismay.

'Really,' he said breathlessly, 'the place is unsafe. One of these days, the entire structure will fall down. If that should happen while some of the children from the village are playing about here it could be very serious — very serious indeed.'

But Sergeant Leek wasn't listening. The fall of brick had dislodged an old and rusty ventilator that had been fixed above the window, and wedged in the broken grill was a small packet wrapped in tattered brown paper.

'Hold this torch, will you?' said Leek, thrusting his torch into the rector's hand. 'Show the light on here.'

'What is it?' asked the Reverend Oswald Hornbeam as he complied. 'What have you found?'

'I don't know yet,' answered the lean sergeant, husky with the excitement that was welling up within him, 'but I think it's what I've been lookin' for.'

With fingers that shook in spite of his efforts to keep them steady, he carefully detached the packet from the rusty ventilator. The paper wrapping was wet with damp and covered with mildew.

Leek gently tore it away and then stared in dismay at what he found.

It was a very old copy of a book of children's nursery rhymes.

★ ★ ★

Mr. Budd listened without comment until Leek had finished recounting his adventures of the evening.

'Well, you *have* been enjoyin' yourself, haven't you?' he said scathingly. 'Now, I s'pose it'll be all over the village that the police are lookin' for hidden treasure in Jackson's Folly.'

'At least I found somethin',' answered Leek defensively.

Mr. Budd grunted.

'A child's book of nursery rhymes,' he retorted. 'An' you nearly knocked the 'ouse down to find it.'

He picked up the tattered book which Leek had brought back and looked at it disparagingly.

'It may be an important clue,' said the lean sergeant. 'It ties up with them rhymes on the door . . .'

'So do over a million copies of the same book,' remarked Mr. Budd. 'That's about as many of this as there are in existence, I should say. Prob'ly more . . . '

'But why should this have been hidden in the ventilator?' demanded the sergeant. 'Made into a packet an' wrapped up in brown paper?'

The stout superintendent eyed him pityingly.

'I s'pose it hasn't occured to your limited intelligence,' he said, 'that this old house has been the principle playground for the village children for years? Can't you use your imagination and think how it got there?'

'You mean it was one of the children . . . ?' began Leek.

'Of course,' interrupted Mr. Budd. 'Anybody but you would've guessed that straight away . . . '

Leek shook his head.

'I'm not sure you're right,' he said. 'This thing could be some sort o' code.'

'Left by the feller that was dropped to spy?' said Mr. Budd. 'Now you're lettin' your imagination run away with you. I

144

shouldn't think it was a bit likely. Anyway, it wouldn't've anything to do with this business.'

Leek was loath to have his discovery treated so cavalierly, but he knew from experience that it was useless to argue with Mr. Budd.

'What does interest me,' remarked the big man, after a moments pause, 'is this business of the Reverend Oswald Hornbeam.'

'What business?' asked Leek in surprise.

'Why, his suddenly turnin' up like that,' said Mr. Budd, frowning. 'Now that strikes me as both interestin' an' peculiar.'

'He saw me light — I told you,' explained the sergeant.

'That's what he said,' remarked Mr. Budd thoughtfully. 'Do you believe that if 'e'd seen a light in that house, he'd've risked comin' to see what it was?' He shook his head doubtfully. 'I don't think he would. Knowin' what had happened there, I don't think one person out of a hundred would.'

'What do you think he came for, then?' asked the sergeant.

'I don't know,' answered the stout superintendent. 'But I've got an idea that he didn't know there was anybody in the buildin'. When he found you was there, he had to make some excuse, an' the light was the best he could think of.'

Leek blinked at the other in sheer astonishment.

'You're not suggestin' that the rector's mixed up in this business, are you?' he said.

'I don't know who's mixed up in it,' said Mr. Budd wearily. 'So if I believe everybody is, I can't be far wrong. There's that schoolteacher woman, Titmarsh. She's afraid of somethin' an' she knew who Sprigot was before anybody else, except the police. How did she know? I'd like to be able to answer that — an' a good few other things as well. The thing we've got to do is to find some sort of a kickin' off place. That's what we've got to do, an' I don't mind admittin' that I can't think of anythin' at the moment. I've come up against some pretty queer cases

146

in me time, but this is the queerest, bar none.'

It was completely inexplicable and chaotic. Nothing that by the wildest stretch of the imagination could be called a clue had come to light. Mr. Budd had more or less discarded his original vague idea that there might be something of value at Jackson's Folly which Sam Sprigot had got to hear about and had taken. He couldn't make it fit in with all the rest. Again and again he returned to that three months hiatus in the little crook's life immediately after he had been released from prison. He had a hunch that here was the starting point he was in search of, if he could only find out where Sam Sprigot had gone and what he had been doing.

Long after the disappointed Leek had gone to solace himself with further notes for his autobiography, the big man lay on his bed thinking.

It was late when the idea came to him suddenly.

Harry Bates!

He was annoyed that he hadn't thought

of Harry before. If anybody could help him, Harry could. Harry knew everything that went on in that sub-stratum of life which is usually referred to as the underworld.

Mr. Budd decided that he would go up to London the first thing on the following morning and seek out Harry. Having made up his mind, he undressed, got into bed, and was soon sleeping the sleep of the just.

12

There is, in a side turning off the Tottenham Court Road, a rather dingy restaurant known colloquially, and for no known reason, to its customers as 'Spotties'. It is owned and presided over by an Italian called Monelli, who appears to have absorbed so much of the oil in which he cooks his dishes that he has now reached saturation point for he is continually bedewed with greasy drops.

Casual customers are not welcomed at 'Spotties'. It caters almost exclusively for those known both to Mr. Monelli and each other, and in this respect is somewhat like a club. Strangers are looked at with suspicion and are treated with such off-hand rudeness that they seldom come again.

And yet 'Spotties' is nearly always full, for here come regularly the flotsam and jetsam of crookdom to plot and plan and compare notes, and many a hold-up, smash and grab, or other illegal enterprise, has had its genesis over spaghetti and coffee in the non-too-clean room behind the snack-counter at the entrance.

It was nearly mid-day when Mr. Budd, in accordance with his decision of the previous night, entered this establishment and approached the proprietor behind the counter.

''Lo, Monelli,' he greeted. 'I'm lookin' for Harry Bates. Is he here?'

Mr. Monelli, fat, greasy, and with his obese figure enveloped in a dirty apron, rubbed the thick hair on his bare forearm, and looked wary.

'I 'ave not seen 'im for one, two, t'ree days,' he answered.

'You can tell the truth,' said Mr. Budd genially, 'I don't want him for anythin'. I only want a word with him about Sam. You remember Sam Sprigot?'

Mr. Monelli nodded.

'Of course, you do,' said Mr. Budd. 'Old customer of yours, eh? Well now, what about Harry?'

Mr. Monelli jerked a dirty thumb toward the inner sanctum. He said nothing but the action required no explaining. Mr. Budd moved ponderously through the curtained arch that led into the restaurant portion of the establishment.

The place was shaped like an L. In the main part a dozen or so small tables left a narrow aisle between them, and they were nearly all occupied. At the appearance of Mr. Budd there was a sudden dead silence, a hush of almost dreadful expectancy.

'It's all right, boys,' said the stout superintendent. 'You can carry on happily. This is a friendly visit.' He caught sight of a thin, pale-faced little man at a corner table. 'Hello, Sniffy. I'll give you a word of advice, while I'm 'ere. I wouldn't pull that job at Matson's shop, if I was you?'

He smiled and passed on and Sniffy Sleator wiped a suddenly damp face. How had the old so-and-so known that he was planning to bust Matson's the tobacconists? He hastily revised his plans and thanked his stars for the warning.

Mr. Budd turned the angle and found

151

himself in the smaller portion of the restaurant. There were only three tables here, set in shallow alcoves, and the man he was looking for was sitting at one of them, a cup of coffee in front of him, studying the racing edition of an evening paper.

He looked up as Mr. Budd stopped by the table.

'Well, look who's 'ere,' he exclaimed. 'I aint seen you for ages.'

'You nearly did, Harry — about three weeks ago,' remarked the big man, pulling up a vacant chair and lowering himself gingerly into it. 'However, we'll let that pass. I'm in search of information.'

A shadow passed over the broad, good-looking face of Mr. Bates.

'I'm no squealer,' he muttered.

'You were a pretty good friend of Sam Sprigot's, wasn't you?' inquired Mr. Budd.

'Poor old Sam,' said Harry Bates, shaking his head. 'I read about that in the papers. Who did him in?'

'I don't know — not yet,' said Mr. Budd.

'Queer business, eh?' said the other. 'You on it?'

'Yes, I believe you can help. I'm hopin' you can . . .'

Mr. Monelli came through with a cup of coffee which he set down in front of the big man.

'On the 'ouse,' he said briefly and departed.

Harry Bates grinned.

'Not often 'e does that,' he remarked. 'Break 'is heart to give anything away. I don't see how I can help you — about Sam. I don't know anything about it . . .'

There was a wary expression in his small, dark eyes that convinced Mr. Budd that he was lying.

'I'll tell you what I want to know, Harry,' he said, leaning forward across the table and lowering his voice. 'Did you see or hear anything from Sam after he came out of stir?'

Harry Bates pushed aside his newspaper, fumbled in his pocket, took out a packet of cigarettes, stuck one between his rather thick lips, and lit. He performed these actions with great deliberation.

153

'Sam was a friend of yours, wasn't he?' prompted Mr. Budd gently. 'You'd like to know that the person what killed him was goin' to pay for it, wouldn't you? It wasn't a nice killin', you know.'

Harry blew out a cloud of smoke. His small eyes surveyed Mr. Budd shrewdly.

'I liked old Sam,' he said after a pause. 'He was a good feller. I can't tell you much because I don't know much, but I'll tell you what I do know.'

The big man pulled his chair a little closer to the table.

'Not here,' said Harry Bates. 'D'you know that little teashop in Oxford Street — it's just past the news theatre?'

Mr. Budd nodded.

'You go along there an' wait for me,' said Harry. 'I'll be along in five or ten minutes.'

He picked up his paper and leaned back in his chair. Mr. Budd got up.

'So long, Harry,' he said and walked ponderously towards the exit.

'You finds him?' asked Mr. Monelli, drying a cup from a stack on the counter.

'You know I did,' answered Mr. Budd.

154

'Might as well've saved meself the trouble.'

Mr. Monelli shrugged his fat shoulders. 'These fellers,' he said. 'Like childers.'

Mr. Budd thought there wasn't very much that was childlike about the customers who frequented Mr. Monelli's establishment, but he kept the thought to himself, wished the proprietor good morning, and went out into the street. Two men who saw him leave the restaurant crossed hastily over to the other side of the road.

The stout superintendent had no difficulty in finding the teashop that Harry had mentioned, but there was a long string of people waiting to go in.

Mr. Budd frowned. It was the lunch hour. There wouldn't be much chance of getting in here, and even if he did there would be no chance at all of talking to Harry and finding out what he had to tell. The only thing he could do was to wait until Harry Bates arrived and try and find another rendezvous. There was a pub on the corner a few doors up the street. That might do.

It wasn't long before he saw Harry threading his way through the crowds on the pavement and went to meet him.

'I ought to have thought about its bein' lunch time,' he said, when Mr. Budd explained the predicament. 'All right, let's go into the pub. You go along first. I don't want to be seen talking to you. It'll get me a bad reputation.'

The saloon bar was full, but there was plenty of room in one corner away from the bar. Mr. Budd ordered two pints of bitter and carried them over to a small table. Most of the customers were grouped at the bar, laughing and chattering, and there would be nobody near enough to overhear what they were saying.

In a few seconds, Harry Bates came in, gave a swift glance round to assure himself that there was nobody he knew, and joined Mr. Budd in the corner. He set the chair carefully, before sitting down, so that he had his back to the bar.

'Now, Harry,' said the big man. 'Let's hear what you've got to say.'

Harry took a long drink, set down his

glass, and leaned forward.

'You're goin' to be disappointed,' he said in a low voice. 'I can't tell you very much. When Sam came out of stir, he phoned me. He hadn't much money an' he wanted to borrow some, see? Sam was all right about that. If you lent him money you could be sure of gettin' it back. I arranged to see him at Victoria, under the clock. He wouldn't go to 'Spotties' or any of the other places. Under the clock at Victoria, he said an' nothin' 'ud shift him. Sam was an obstinate bloke an' I knew it was no good arguin', so at eight that evenin' I went along — eight was the time he'd arranged. There was no sign of Sam when I got there an' he didn't turn up until twenty minutes past.

'You're lucky I'm still here,' I said. 'Another coupla minutes an' I was goin'.' 'I couldn't get along before,' he said. 'I got held up.' He was fidgety an' excited, kept on lookin' over his shoulder, an' eyein' all the people that was passin'. I suggested we should go along to one of the buffets an' have a drink. Sam agreed, though I thought he seemed a bit reluctant, and when we was drinkin' a coupla scotches I handed him over the money he'd asked for — twenty pounds.

'Thanks, Harry,' he said. 'I'll let you have this back in a week or two.'

'Got any plans?' I asked and he looked at me queerly over the top of his glass.

'I'm on to somethin' really big,' he said seriously. 'The biggest thing I've ever got hold of.'

'What are you goin' to do?' I said jokingly, 'rob the Bank of England?'

'It's got nothin' to do with robbery,' he answered. 'It's somethin' I stumbled on by accident. It frightens me a bit . . . '

'He looked scared. His hands were tremblin' a bit an' his eyes were shiftin' all over the place. I tried to get him to tell me more about it, but he wouldn't. 'I got to be careful,' he said, 'but I'll tell you this, Harry. I won't have to bother with climbin' pipes no more. I'll be livin' in luxury for the rest o' me life.' That's all I could get out of him an' that was the last I ever saw of him.'

'Or hear from him?' asked Mr. Budd.

'No, I heard from him,' said Harry

Bates. 'About a month later, it was. He sent back the twenty quid with a short note — only a few lines. 'I'll be seein' you soon, Harry an' many thanks. I'll be amongst the aristocracy when you hear from me again. Good luck. Sam.' That was all. I didn't see or hear anythin' more from him. The next thing I knew about him was that he'd been murdered.'

Harry Bates finished his beer, and Mr. Budd frowned. He hadn't learnt very much but at least it advanced him that tiny bit further. Sam Sprigot had discovered something that he thought was going to bring him in a lot of money. It sounded to the big man like blackmail.

'I s'pose,' he said, 'you didn't see where this note with the money was posted?'

'Greystock,' answered Harry.

Greystock. The nearest town to the village of Marbury.

So that night, when someone had ended Sam Sprigot's dreams of unlimited wealth in the old ruin of Jackson's Folly, had *not* been the little crooks first visit to the neighbourhood. He had, at least for sufficiently long to post a letter, been in

159

Greystock. Had he been there during the whole period of those missing three months? If so why had he gone back to London and taken lodgings with Mrs. Bagley? And what was this stupendous thing he had accidentally discovered, which, in his own words, had 'frightened him a bit'? That remark in his note to Harry Bates about the aristocracy. Could that have referred to the Conyers?

'An' Sam never gave you any inkling of what this thing was 'e had discovered?' said Mr. Budd.

Harry Bates shook his head.

'Not a thing,' he declared. 'Close as an' oyster over it. I've told you all he told me.'

But he hadn't. Long experience had taught Mr. Budd to know when a person was lying. It had become a kind of sixth sense. And he was pretty sure that Harry Bates knew something that he had *not* divulged concerning the late Mr. Sam Sprigot's aspirations to wealth.

13

After leaving Harry Bates, Mr. Budd got on a bus and was taken with more or less swiftness to Whitehall. During the journey his mind was busily occupied with what he had just learnt, and there was a very thoughtful expression on his heavy face as he turned in at the entrance to Scotland Yard, nodded to the man on duty, and slowly walked up the stairs to his room. Going into his bare, cheerless office, he hung up his hat, sat down behind the desk, and clasping his hands over his capacious stomach, leaned back in his chair and closed his eyes.

Anyone who might have looked in the room would have thought that the stout man was asleep, but they would have been very far from the truth. The alert brain behind the bovine appearance and slowness of speech, which many people had discounted to their subsequent undoing, was busy worrying like a ferret at the problem which its owner was trying to solve.

The big man had not brought the mournful Leek with him from Marbury, a fact for which the sergeant had been very thankful. He preferred the peace and quietness of Kenwiddy's farm.

For nearly an hour, Mr. Budd remained lost in his thoughts, and then he roused himself, lit one of his atrocious black cigars, and picking up the house telephone asked to be put through to an extension number.

A few seconds after he had hung up the receiver, there was a tap on the office door, and a youngish man of nondescript appearance came in.

'Sit down, Willit,' said Mr. Budd, and Detective Constable Willit perched himself on the edge of a chair. 'D'you know a feller called Harry Bates?'

The other nodded.

'Used to be mixed up in the tipster racket,' he said. 'Goes in mostly for small racing swindles. He was in that greyhound doping business . . . '

'That's the feller,' said Mr. Budd. 'Now, I want him tailed. I want him tailed night an' day an' a full report of where 'e goes an' who he sees.'

'Okay,' said Willit.

'They'll give you full particulars about him in Records,' went on the stout superintendent, 'where 'e lives an' his usual haunts. I want you to get onto it at once. Your relief 'ull be arranged for. I want to know everythin' that feller does from now on, understand?'

Detective Constable Willit said he understood very well and departed.

Mr. Budd brushed the ash from the front of his waistcoat and went along to see the assistant commissioner.

Colonel Blair, as dapper and neat as usual, looked up as the big man came in.

'Hello, Budd,' he greeted. 'I was just thinking about you. I thought you were at Marbury.'

Mr. Budd explained the reason why he was not.

'I see,' remarked the assistant commissioner, twiddling a pencil between his fingers. 'Difficult case, eh?'

'Very, sir,' answered the stout superintendent. 'There's practically nothin' to go on. I'm hopin' that Harry Bates may give us a line.'

'You think he knows something he hasn't told you?' said Colonel Blair, 'Well, you may be right. What other lines are you following up?'

'Two,' answered Mr. Budd. 'I want a detailed report on Sam Sprigot. Who his parents was, where 'e was born, everything about him. An' I'd like the same thing with Sir Basil an' Lady Conyers, sir.'

Colonel Blair made a brief note on a pad at his elbow.

'I'll have that attended to,' he said. 'It shouldn't take very long.'

'There was a brother, sir — Francis Conyers. He blotted his copy book some years ago over a forged cheque, or somethin' of the sort. I'd like to know all about that.'

The assistant commissioner scrawled another note.

'Where is he now?' he asked.

'Nobody seems to know, sir,' replied

Mr. Budd. 'He disappeared after this cheque business, or whatever-it-was, and nobody's seen or heard of him since.'

'And, I suppose, he's now the heir to the estate, eh?' said Colonel Blair. 'Um, yes. I see the line you're working on there. Anything else?'

'Well, sir,' said Mr. Budd, 'there is one other thing. It seems that durin' the war, the Germans dropped a feller in Marbury by parachute. This feller injured his leg in landin' an' had to hide up in Jackson's Folly . . . '

Colonel Blair's eyes narrowed.

'Jackson's Folly, eh?' he said. 'Where Sprigot and Conyers were killed.'

'Yes, sir,' agreed Mr. Budd. 'I don't think there's any connection . . . '

'You're quite right not to neglect anything,' interrupted the assistant commissioner.

'He was captured by the Home Guard before he could get in touch with his 'contact',' said Mr. Budd. 'Now, what I'd like to know is what happened to this feller, who 'e was, an' whether the contact was ever found.'

Colonel Blair made a third note.

'I'll get on to M.I.5 and ask them to look up their records,' he said. 'It's a long time ago but I expect they'll still be able to let us have the information. You know, this is a queer business, Superintendent, and the queerest thing about it is that recurring nursery rhyme. Have you any theory to account for that?'

Mr. Budd shook his head.

'I haven't any theory to account for anything, sir,' he replied candidly. 'I'm just flounderin' about in the dark tryin' to get hold of something.'

'Which you usually do,' said Colonel Blair with a smile. 'I'm quite happy to leave the matter in your hands. You always pull something out of the bag in the end.'

Mr. Budd was not feeling so optimistic as he went back to his office, But still, he had set a few wheels turning. Maybe, from the various results that would accrue there would be, as he had said, 'something to get hold of'.

★   ★   ★

Mr. Harry Bates finished his coffee, lighted a cigarette, and sat at the stained table in 'Spotties' smoking thoughtfully. He was trying to make up his mind on a course of action that had been hovering in his brain ever since he had read of the murder of his friend, Sam Sprigot.

The unexpected interview with Mr. Budd had rather taken him by surprise. He had not been prepared for that but, he hoped, that he had satisfied the stout superintendent with what he had told him.

Up to a point what he had said had been the truth. It was what he had *not* said — what he had kept back — that was the cause of his deep cogitation. For Sam had revealed a little more than he, Harry Bates, had told the big man. It was a very little, but it might, if it was handled properly, prove to be profitable.

The question that was troubling him at the moment was the best way to handle it.

Harry was no fool. The business in which Sam had got himself involved was dangerous. There was no doubt about that. The fact that Sam was dead was sufficient proof that it was dangerous, but there might be quite a lot to be got out of it — if it was handled right.

That was the crux of the whole thing — to handle it right.

He finished his cigarette and lighted another.

He was under no illusions regarding what Mr. Budd would do. He wouldn't just accept his word that he had told him all he knew. He was too cute for that. So what would he do? He'd have him watched, that's what he'd do. Somebody 'ud be put on to tail him and that somebody would have to be shaken off before Harry could put into practice the idea which was then taking shape in his mind.

That would be fairly easy. Harry Bates had more than once succeeded in dodging a possible tailer . . .

He looked at his watch. It was a little after six o'clock. He got up, said goodnight to the greasy Mr. Monelli behind the counter and went out into the street, strolling slowly off in the direction of Oxford Street. Without appearing to be the least interested, his eyes were vigilently on the look out for possible tailers, and he soon spotted the man who was casually walking along in his wake.

The same man had been on the other side of the road when he had come out of Spotties.

To make sure, Harry negotiated a number of side turnings, walking at the same leisurely pace. The man behind him was still there, at almost the same distance in his rear, when he once more came back to the main thoroughfare.

Harry smiled to himself. He continued on his way up Oxford Street until he reached the Circus. Here he paused on the edge of the pavement waiting for the traffic to stop so that he could cross the road. At least this was the impression he wished to give to the tailer. Out of the corner of his eye he saw, at last, what he was waiting for — a taxi for hire. He signalled the driver and before the man had time to pull up, had opened the door and jumped inside with a muttered 'Victoria Station'.

The taxi gathered speed as Harry slumped down in a corner. After a moment or two, he cautiously looked out the little window at the back. Another taxi was speeding along in their wake. It was going fast and could easily have overtaken them but a few yards behind it slowed and, adjusting its speed to the other, followed behind.

Harry Bates smiled to himself. The 'tail' had been lucky. There must have been another empty cab almost immediately behind the one he had got. Oh, well, he could elude the follower at Victoria. It ought to be easy.

He leaned back in the seat, fumbled in his pocket for his cigarettes, and lighted one. There was nothing he could do now until they reached Victoria.

Presently the cab swung into the front of the station and stopped. Harry got out, taking his time to search for his fare, paid the driver, and strolled into the busy station. In a mirror that was fastened to a wall, he saw the man who had been outside Monelli's walking slowly along in his rear.

Harry went over to the Surburban Line ticket office and bought a ticket for Battersea Park. As he moved over to the platform from which the train went he saw his tailer at the ticket office window. Harry sauntered onto the platform. The train wasn't in yet and he waited patiently, walking up and down humming a tune.

After a few minutes the train drew in and Harry was almost the first to board it. He chose an empty compartment, slipped quickly to the opposite door, opened it and dropped onto the line. A few seconds later, unseen by anyone, he had pulled himself up onto the other platform, hurried out of the station by the News Theatre entrance, and, hailing the first taxi was driven to Waterloo.

There was no sign of anyone on his tail this time and he congratulated himself that he had succeeded in fobbing off the watcher.

Having made doubly certain at Waterloo that the tailer was no longer in evidence, he took a ticket to Marbury . . .

Miss Titmarsh finished her frugal supper, washed up the dishes in her neat little sink, and made herself a cup of tea. Carrying this into the sitting room, she fetched a thick bundle of exercise books from a table, put them on her desk and began to mark them.

This was her usual nightly occupation and it took her until it was time for her to go to bed.

She still felt far from well. The headache which had been so troublesome recently was still hovering in the background, ready to leap out in full fettle at the slightest provocation. Miss Titmarsh had kept it at bay during the past few days with aspirin until she dreaded to think of the number she must have taken.

Half way through the pile of books, she paused and rubbed her eyes. It was a monotonous job, checking and marking. She leaned back in her hard chair to rest her back.

She was just going on with her task when there came a knock on the front door. She looked at the little clock on the mantelpiece. It was half-past nine. Who could it be at this hour?

The knock was repeated a little louder. Miss Titmarsh got up. Perhaps it was someone from the village about one of the children . . . She put on the dim light in the tiny hall and cautiously opened the front door.

A man stood on the step — a man in a heavy overcoat. A complete stranger to Miss Titmarsh.

'Miss Titmarsh?' he inquired in a voice that had a twang in it — not at all an educated voice.

'Yes,' answered Miss Titmarsh. 'What is it? What do you want?'

'I should like to have a talk to you, Miss,' said the stranger. His manner was quite pleasant but Miss Titmarsh felt vaguely uneasy.

'Are you — are you from the police?' she asked doubtfully.

Harry Bates laughed.

'Well, not exactly,' he answered. 'The police an' me couldn't be called pals, not by a long chalk.'

'Then what do you want with me?' she asked. 'I don't know you . . . '

'You knew a friend of mine,' he retorted. 'You knew him quite well. Sam . . . Sam Sprigot.'

Miss Titmarsh put out her hand quickly and gripped the door post to steady herself. She felt the blood receding from her brain and the resultant dizziness.

'I — I don't know what you mean,' she whispered faintly. 'That was the name of the man who — who was killed here . . . '

'That's right,' said Harry Bates.

'I knew nothing about him,' said Miss Titmarsh, gripping the door frame tighter. 'I — I never knew him . . . '

'Don't try an' pull that stuff on me,' said Harry. 'Sam talked to me about you — not so very long before he was murdered. I know all about you, see?'

'You — you'd better come in,' said Miss Titmarsh breathlessly. 'You'd better come in . . . '

'That's fine,' agreed Harry. 'You an' me have got a lot to talk about.'

Miss Titmarsh said nothing. She was

incapable of saying anything. Her throat was dry and the pain in her head had suddenly come on again with agonizing stabs that seemed to cut through to the centre of her brain.

It had come. The thing she had dreaded had come at last . . .

She led the way into her little sitting room unsteadily.

'Will you sit down, please?' she said.

Mr. Bates carefully removed his coat, folded it over the back of a chair, and sat down. Taking a packet of cigarettes from his pocket he lit one and blew the smoke gently up to the ceiling.

Miss Titmarsh also sat down, in the extreme centre of her small settee.

'What have you come here for?' she asked after a pause.

'I want to talk to you about Sam,' answered Harry Bates. 'I don't know quite how to address you, you know. Shall I call you Miss Titmarsh or — Mrs. Sprigot?'

She caught her breath with a sharp sound — a curious rattle as though her throat was full of dried leaves. Her hands, folded in her lap, twisted convulsively.

'I have been known by the name of Titmarsh for many years,' she said at last. 'It was my maiden name. Everybody knows me as Miss Titmarsh . . . '

'You can remain Miss Titmarsh, so far as I'm concerned. I'm not fussy,' said Harry. 'What's in a name, after all? The whole question is that Sam came to see you a month or so before he was murdered, didn't he?'

She nodded. She would never forget the night she had gone to the door and found her husband on the step . . . Those headaches had dated from the moment . . .

'What did he come for?' asked Harry. 'He didn't come just to say 'hello', did he? You an' he hadn't met for years — not since you left him an' came to live here.'

Miss Titmarsh passed the tip of her tongue over dry lips and swallowed with difficulty.

'What did he tell you?' repeated Harry Bates. 'He was on to somethin' big an' he wanted you to help him. What was it?'

She looked at him with troubled eyes.

The pain in her head was getting worse, and she put up a thin hand and pressed her temple to try and ease it. But still she said nothing.

'You'd better tell me, you know,' persisted Harry. His voice was quite gentle but behind the gentleness there lurked a threat. 'You don't want your connection with Sam to get around, do you? It wouldn't do you any good in this place, you know. You'd lose your job. They wouldn't like the widow of a crook like Sam to teach their children, would they?'

'You — you wouldn't . . . ?' Miss Titmarsh's voice trailed away.

'I don't want to do anything — unpleasant,' said Mr. Bates. 'But I'm going to know just what Sam had in his mind. All you've got to do is to tell me. Then you needn't worry any more . . . '

Miss Titmarsh made up her mind.

'Very well,' she said.

14

Mr. Budd was notified that the tailer had lost track of Harry Bates at Victoria Station, and said a great deal that was not fit for publication. The recipient of these caustic observations was reduced to inarticulate apologies that only produced a further stream of invective from the stout superintendent. But the fact remained. Harry Bates had succeeded in reaching his unknown destination without anybody but himself being the wiser.

After the trouble he had taken to insure that Harry should be kept under observation, it was not surprising that the big man should feel annoyed.

He sat in the dining room at Kenwiddy's farm, chewing on one of his unlighted cigars, and in a mood that was only describable as foul. Leek, after trying to soothe him down, and getting the overflow of his temper, fled to his own room and sought solace in the grubby exercise book containing the notes for his autobiography.

The post, which was intermittent in Marbury, arrived just before mid-day and there was a bulky envelope for Mr. Budd which did a little to cheer him up. It contained the dossier of Sam Sprigot, and everything that was discoverable concerning the Conyers.

After the enormous lunch provided by Mrs. Kenwiddy, Mr. Budd carried these documents up to his room, locked the door, lay down comfortably on his bed, and began systematically to peruse them.

He began with the record of Sam Sprigot. The early part of the little crook's life was rather sketchy. His father had, apparently, been a respectable motor mechanic and his mother had worked in a shop. Sam had left school at the age of fourteen and had had a succession of different jobs, none of which he had remained at very long. He had got in with a lot of undesirable companions and had, before he was sixteen, twice been in Court for stealing from shops. His first serious conviction was for breaking and entering a tobacconists shop and stealing cigarettes. After he had served his sentence for this offence, he had gone straight for a period of nearly twelve months during which time it was believed that he had married a woman who was a teacher in a Council School at Hither Green . . .

Mr. Budd paused when he reached this. A schoolteacher? His mind conjured up a picture of Miss Titmarsh. She had known the identity of Sam Sprigot before it had become public property. She was definitely afraid of something . . . Could it be that *she* was the person Sam had married? Remembering her, it seemed unlikely but people changed. Maybe at that time she was quite a goodlooking girl. But why should she now call herself 'Miss' Titmarsh? That was easy. If she had discovered what Sam was, and disapproved, she had probably left him . . .

It would be simple to make sure. The marriage certificate would contain her maiden name which was the most likely one she would have gone back to. Mr. Budd made a mental note to have this looked up. If she had been Sam Sprigot's wife it would account for a lot.

Perhaps she might know where he had spent that three months that were unaccounted for and be able to give some clue as to why he had gone, that night when somebody had struck him down, to the old, ruined house?

It was definitely an idea. Of course, the schoolteacher might just be a coincidence. There must be thousands of schoolteachers who could have been the one who had married Sprigot, but it was worth following up.

There was nothing much more of interest in 'Stack-pipe' Sam's record. Mr. Budd read through the list of his various operations without discovering anything that was likely to help in the present case, and turned his attention to the history of the Conyers.

Sir Thomas Conyers, the father of Basil and Francis, had married twice. His first marriage had been to Millicent Harrington who had presented him with two children — the two already named. After her death — she had apparently been killed in a train accident — Sir Thomas had married a Mrs. Harriet Levington, a widow with one daughter, Isobel, the present Mrs. Mortlock. She had married James Mortlock at the age of twenty-six. It had proved an unhappy marriage. Apparently her husband drank heavily, left her after four years of unhappiness and misery, and departed abroad with another woman, where he died shortly afterwards in extreme poverty.

This, thought Mr. Budd, would account for Mrs. Mortlock's rather warped outlook on the world in general.

The two brothers, Basil and Francis, had both been educated at the same preparatory school and gone to Oxford. There was only a matter of eighteen months difference in their ages, but a great deal of difference in their temperament. Francis had always been rather wild and had neither distinguished himself at school, or later at the university. Basil, never a very bright scholar had, however, managed to scrape through with a certain amount of reputation, if not for brilliance at least for diligence.

A few years before old Sir Thomas died from a stroke, Francis had got into hot water over money. Heavily in debt, and with his creditors pressing him on all sides, he had forged a cheque in his father's name and cleared out of the country. That was the last that had ever been seen or heard of him. Where he had gone nobody knew, but he had taken three thousand pounds with him, leaving the creditors high and dry and screaming for his blood. Old Sir Thomas, for the sake of the family name, had settled his debts. It was a fit of temper due to his discovery of what Francis had done that had contributed to the stroke from which he subsequently died.

Basil was on holiday in Switzerland when the news of his father's death reached him and he came back to claim the estate. A year later, he had met and married Sybil Marsden, an attractive woman in her early thirties, with a large fortune left her by her uncle, whom he had met at a cocktail party in London. They had settled in Marbury, and Sir Basil had proceeded to get rid of his fortune as quickly as possible on racing and women. At the time of his death there was very little left of his own money, although, since his wife had predeceased him, if only by a very short period, he had died a rich man, her fortune having passed to him as next of kin.

Mr. Budd frowned.

Was there anything in this history that helped to shed a light on the reason for the murders? In the case of Lady Conyers the person who benefited by her death was obviously her husband. But he had himself been killed shortly after. Was his death connected with the murder of Sam Sprigot but not with the murder of Lady Conyers? The method in her case was different. Poison.

The stout superintendent reached for one of his cigars, lit it, and blew a cloud of acrid smoke toward the ceiling.

Suppose you looked at it this way. Suppose, for the sake of argument, you took Lady Conyers's death as a separate thing — as quite apart from the other murders? What did you get then?

Mr. Budd shook his head.

There was the writing on the door against that theory. Another bit out of the same nursery rhyme that had been used on the paper pinned to the door of Jackson's Folly. And both written in blue pencil. That seemed to prove that the same person was responsible for both . . .

Hold on, though. Did it?

Supposing somebody had *wanted* it thought that the same person was responsible for both murders? What then? Well, *what* then? The poison had been put in Lady Conyers's glass of water before Sam had even *reached* Marbury much less been killed. So that was a wash-out . . .

Or was it? Could the murderer have already planned Sam's death when he, or she, had put the poison in Lady Conyers's glass?

That was possible but it meant that the murderer of Sam Sprigot and the murderer of Lady Conyers was one and the same person. That was all right — if the murderer was Sir Basil. How did that fit?

Mr. Budd frowned.

It fitted quite well — except that Sir Basil himself had been a victim. And that upset the apple cart.

The big man raised a ponderous hand and scratched his chin. It really was the toughest case he'd ever had anything to do with. You just couldn't get your teeth into it anywhere. If you thought you'd found a soft bit it turned hard on you before you could take a good bite. And yet there must be a solution if only you could get the right end of it — a solution in which all the disconnected parts would drop into place and fit neatly . . .

Perhaps he was looking at the whole problem from the wrong angle. Was there any other way of tackling it? Supposing, instead of starting from Sam Sprigot's murder, you started from Lady Conyers death? What happened then?

Mr. Budd closed his eyes and drew his brows together in a concentrated frown.

And suddenly something did happen. Something remarkable happened. An idea that was startling in its simplicity suddenly came out of nowhere as such ideas do. The various bits of the puzzle settled neatly into place — that is with the exception of one. That one was quite a large one but it might be persuaded to fall into position when the whole thing was reviewed carefully.

The stout superintendent opened his eyes, took a deep pull at his cigar and slowly exhaled the smoke.

There was a lot of thinking still to be done — a lot of marshalling of facts already in his possession and several facts to be found — but the main outline of the idea was sound.

At first glance it seemed fantastic but when you came to examining it it was quite reasonable. It made sense . . .

The big man got heavily off the bed.

At last he had discovered what he had been looking for — a jumping off point . . .

★   ★   ★

Roger Marsden looked at Mr. Titer and Mr. Titer looked up at the ceiling.

They were in the big drawing room at Marbury Court Roger perched on the arm of an easy chair, the solicitor standing in front of the fireplace.

'So Sybil's money goes with the estate?' said Roger.

Mr. Titer, who had just informed him of this fact, nodded.

Roger got up and walked over to the french window. Resting his hand on the edge of the frame he looked out at the deserted terrace.

'Who inherits?' he asked without turning his head.

Mr. Titer, who strongly objected to answering a direct question, coughed.

'At the — er — present juncture,' he answered reluctantly, 'it would seem that — er — that the late Sir Basil's step-sister will inherit. Unless, of course, we can establish that Francis Conyers is still alive . . . '

'That's going to take some time,' said Roger. He came back and resumed his position on the arm of the chair.

'Yes,' agreed Mr. Titer. 'There are difficulties — a number of difficulties.' He sighed.

'There wasn't much of Basil's money

left, was there?' inquired Roger.

Mr. Titer frowned. He disliked these questions. He disliked any question that could be plainly answered.

'I'm afraid Sir Basil's fortune was sadly depleted,' he replied after a pause. 'Sadly depleted.'

'How much was there left?' said Roger.

The lawyer shifted uneasily.

'That will have to be gone into,' he answered evasively. 'Not a great deal, but I am not prepared to state exactly how much.'

'If Basil hadn't been murdered,' remarked Roger, 'he would have been a rich man . . . '

Mr. Titer inclined his head.

'That is so,' he said. 'An exceedingly rich man . . . '

'And so will Francis Conyers be — if he can be found,' said Roger.

'That is so,' said Mr. Titer again.

Roger took out his case, helped himself to a cigarette and lighted it.

'You're advertising for him, I suppose?' he remarked.

Mr. Titer graciously replied once more that 'that was so!'

'And if that doesn't produce results?' asked Roger.

Mr. Titer considered for several seconds before replying.

'In that case we shall have to get the Court to allow us to presume death,' he said. 'Of course, that will be a long business — a very very long business . . .'

'What happens to the estate in the meanwhile?' said Roger.

'We shall, of course, continue to administer that on behalf of the — er — heir or next of kin,' said the solicitor. 'The entire matter is very — er — unfortunate.'

'What are the police doing?' asked Roger. 'So far as I can see they aren't doing much.'

'I've no doubt,' said Mr. Titer, 'that they are persuing all the necessary inquiries. The police are, as a rule, very efficient.'

'Well,' grunted Roger, 'I don't think they've proved so in this particular case. I want to know who was responsible for the death of my sister. I don't care a button about the others, but I was very fond of

190

Sybil and I shan't rest until somebody has been brought to book for putting that poison in her glass of water. It's my private opinion that it was her husband . . .'

Mr. Titer held up a protesting hand and looked extremely shocked.

'Really!' he remonstrated with almost a note of horror in his voice. 'Really, Mr. Marsden, you cannot make these — er — unfounded accusations against people . . .'

'Only one person,' corrected Roger. 'Basil . . .'

'There is no evidence, no evidence at all, to warrant such a thing,' said Mr. Titer.

'There may not be any evidence but it's common sense, all the same,' retorted Roger. 'Basil was broke, or practically broke. He'd gambled his own fortune away . . .'

'That doesn't make him a murderer,' interrupted Mr. Titer. 'Really, I've never heard of such a thing . . .'

'If I know anything of Sybil,' went on Roger, taking no notice of the interruption, 'she wouldn't have let him have a penny of her money while she was alive. She'd have paid all the bills and seen that the estate was kept up and all that, of course, but she wouldn't have given Basil money to chuck away on horses and women. I think my suggestion is pretty reasonable. In fact, evidence or no evidence, I'm convinced that her husband poisoned her to get her money.'

'But he was murdered himself,' said Mr. Titer.

'Yes, I'm aware of that,' agreed Roger, 'but all this business of that little crook at Jackson's Folly and the rest of it may not have anything to do with Sybil's death. That may very easily have been something to do with one of Basil's schemes, you know. He was up to all kinds of tricks . . .'

'I hardly think it could have been one of his schemes to get himself knocked on the head,' remarked the lawyer with a rather wintry smile.

Roger made a grimace.

'No, I'll admit that doesn't fit in,' he said. 'But the rest does. If we could find someone with a motive for killing Basil, I believe that I'm right.'

'You are the only person with a motive for that,' said Mr. Titer shrewdly. 'You were very fond of your sister and if you believed as you say you do, that her husband was responsible for her death . . .'

'You think I might have bashed him over the head?' finished Roger. 'Well, you're quite right!'

Mr. Titer's eyes widened in horrified surprise.

'Are you — are you telling m-me . . . ?' he stuttered, 'that y-y-you . . .'

'I'm not confessing to the murder of Basil, if that's what you mean,' broke in Roger, laughing. 'What I meant was that you were quite right about the motive. If I'd known for certain that it was Basil who killed my sister, I certainly would have murdered him.'

Mr. Titer looked relieved. For the moment he had imagined that the man before him was admitting to murder . . . He took out his handkerchief and wiped his face. Before he could say anything further on the subject, however, the door opened and Mrs. Mortlock came in.

'I hope I'm not interrupting anything,' she said in a tone that suggested she didn't much care whether she was or not, 'but I should like to know when we can leave here, or perhaps I should say when *I* can leave here. That is the thing that interests me most.'

'I'm afraid you will have to ask the officer in charge of the police investigation that, madam,' said Mr. Titer. 'I am — er — not in a position to inform you.'

'I should doubt very much if he would be able to tell anyone anything,' said Mrs. Mortlock shrugging her thin shoulders. 'If you mean that fat man. He always seems to be half asleep to me.'

'Yes, I shouldn't think he was very intelligent,' said Roger, falling into the same error regarding Mr. Budd as a great many people had done before him — to their ultimate cost. 'He seems to be a very stolid, unimaginative sort of man.'

Mr. Titer cleared his throat.

'I am given to understand,' he remarked, 'that Superintendent Budd is one of the Yard's best men.'

Mrs. Mortlock sniffed disparagingly.

'I'm sorry for the others, if that is the case,' she snapped. 'However, the point is how long are we going to be detained here?'

Mr. Titer shook his head.

'That, as I've already told you,' he replied, 'I cannot tell. It's entirely a question for the police . . .'

'Why are you so anxious to get away?' asked Roger.

'I've got my own life to lead,' answered Mrs. Mortlock. 'Now that the whole household here has become disorganized there seems no point in remaining here longer than one can help. Angela, of course, will have to go. There's nothing for her to stay for now that Sybil is dead. I don't know what will happen to Mr. Harper. What is going to be done with the estate?'

Mr. Titer repeated what he had already told Roger Marsden.

'Do you mean that if Francis is proved to be dead, the estate will come to me?' demanded Mrs. Mortlock incredulously. 'To *me*?'

'As the next of kin,' said Mr. Titer, 'I

don't think there is any doubt of it.'

She looked at him and Roger thought there was a slightly dazed expression in her eyes. And yet, he thought, it couldn't have been a complete surprise to her. She must have known that it was a possibility — even more than a possibility.

'There may, of course,' went on the lawyer carefully, 'be a considerable lapse of time before we can — er — definitely hand over the estate to you, but I was going to suggest that you should, in the meanwhile, and pending the necessary legal formalities, take — er — up your residence here and act as — er — steward. You will, naturally require help in the administration of the property and this, of course, we shall be prepared to give you. You could also retain the services of Mr. Harper, whose previous experience would be of value. Would you be prepared to do this?'

Mrs. Mortlock considered.

'I think I should,' she replied at last. 'I'm quite sure that Francis is dead. That was Basil's opinion. Nothing has been heard of him for years . . . '

'If proof of his death can be found it will expedite matters considerably,' said Mr. Titer. 'If we have to go to the Courts to presume death it may, as I told Mr. Marsden, be a rather protracted matter . . . '

'Nobody knew where he went to after he'd forged that cheque,' said Mrs. Mortlock, shaking her head. 'And nobody has heard anything of him since. I should think it would be very difficult to prove that he's dead.'

'I should say he'd turn up quickly enough if he knows that he's heir to the estate,' remarked Roger.

'That depends on whether he sees the advertisement,' said Mr. Titer. 'We shall, of course, have it inserted in the foreign press as well as in America and other English speaking countries. We can only hope that it will bring results. Otherwise . . . ' He shook his head. 'It will be a long business — a long business.'

But it wasn't to be so long as he anticipated. Francis Conyers was to turn up in circumstances that none of them would have dreamed of — even in their wildest imaginings.

15

Harry Bates stirred the cup of tea which Miss Titmarsh had made and looked gloomily at the swirling contents.

'And that's all?' he inquired.

She nodded.

'That's all,' she said.

'I was hoping that he'd told you more,' said Harry. He took a sip of the hot tea. 'He was very excited about something the last time I saw him. 'I'll be independent for life' he said. 'I'm on to a good thing.' But he wouldn't tell me any more . . . '

'He mentioned something of a similar nature to me,' said Miss Titmarsh. 'He said that he would soon be rolling about in his own car. But he was always so untruthful, I didn't take a lot of notice.'

'But he did mention these people up at Marbury Court?' said Harry.

'Yes,' replied Miss Titmarsh reluctantly. 'Yes, he did. He was going to make them pay, he said, a whole lot of money. But he never told me how . . . '

He looked at her with a keen, shrewd glance. Was this prim, school-marmish woman telling the truth? Was she concealing something? He couldn't be sure. She'd concealed the fact of her relationship to Sam pretty well. She might be concealing something else. He wasn't sure, he *couldn't* be sure. But there was nothing much he could do about it. If she chose to deny any knowledge of what Sam had been after he would have to believe her — or, at least, pretend to. He couldn't call her a liar without more definite knowledge.

He drank his tea and got up.

'Well, I suppose I'd better be going,' he said. 'I'm sorry that my visit has been so unprofitable.'

Miss Titmarsh said nothing but he saw the look of relief on her thin face. She too got up and at that moment there came a knock at the front door.

Miss Titmarsh's hand flew up to her flat breast. Her eyes widened with fear and her lips parted.

'Who is it?' whispered Harry Bates,

seeing the look on her face.

Miss Titmarsh shook her head.

'I don't know,' she answered in a voice that was scarcely audible.

'Whoever it is I don't want to be found here,' said Harry. 'Is there a back way?'

Again she shook her head.

'It can be seen from the front porch,' she said in the same low tone. 'Go into the kitchen — through that way.'

She pointed to the door. Harry nodded quickly and she waited until he had disappeared into the little kitchen before she went along the narrow hall and opened the front door.

'Good evenin',' said Mr. Budd. 'I'm sorry to call so late, m'am, but I'd like to have a word with you, if I may.'

Harry Bates, lurking behind the kitchen door, heard the stout superintendent's voice and recognized it. Had the police followed him here after all? Hadn't he been successful in shaking off his tailer? Perhaps there had been more than one?

His jaw tightened as his mouth compressed. He'd no wish for Budd to find him here. Not that there was anything wrong in it but . . . He strained his ears as he heard Miss Titmarsh reply.

'I — I'm just thinking of going to bed,' she said. 'If it isn't anything urgent . . . '

'But I'm afraid it is, m'am,' interrupted Mr. Budd, and the listening Harry wondered why he used the word 'm'am' to a supposed spinster. 'Miss' would have been the right address . . .

Miss Titmarsh had noticed it too. The big man had previously addressed her as 'Miss' . . . Was it just a slip, or did he — *know*?

'I'm afraid it is rather urgent,' repeated Mr. Budd. 'But I shan't keep you long.'

'Very well,' said Miss Titmarsh.

She opened the door wider and Mr. Budd sidled with difficulty into the hall. She led the way into the sitting room, turned and faced him.

'Please tell me as quickly as possible,' she said, 'what it is you want.'

Mr. Budd's sleepy eyes noticed the second cup on the table by the chair and Mr. Budd's sensitive nose smelt the stale cigarette smoke that lingered in the atmosphere. There had been somebody

201

else here recently — very recently for a cigarette end was just smouldering out in the teacup's saucer.

He wondered who the visitor had been and whether he, or she, was still lurking somewhere in the house, but he made no comment.

'I should like to ask you a few questions concernin' the dead man, Sam Sprigot,' he said in his usual sleepy manner, but his eyes, under their half-lowered lids were watchful.

'I know nothing about him — nothing at all,' answered Miss Titmarsh quickly.

But she felt her heart give a sudden jump that made her feel dizzy and faint.

'I don't think that's quite right, is it?' said the stout superintendent slowly. 'I understand that you knew quite a lot about him at one time.'

Miss Titmarsh put out her hand and grasped the back of the chair near which she was standing. How could this man know, she thought.

'I — I don't know what you mean,' she said, and her voice sounded strange and husky even to herself. It might have been somebody else speaking.

'I think you do,' murmured Mr. Budd gently. 'Now, why not admit it, m'am. Sam Sprigot was your husband, wasn't he?'

It was a guess based on that small item in the dead man's record that referred to the 'schoolteacher' but he knew as soon as he saw her face that the shot had gone home.

She made no effort to deny it. Very slowly she nodded.

'Now, m'am,' said Mr. Budd in his most avuncular manner, 'why didn't you tell the police this before? Why did you try and hide up the fact?'

Her eyes, dull and with a queer look behind them of pain, surveyed him almost as though she were blind.

'It wasn't anything to be proud of,' she answered bitterly. 'I have tried to forget it — to keep it from everyone's knowledge. I have always been regarded as respectable here . . . '

Mr. Budd sighed.

Respectable. The motive behind more crimes than he could count. The basis of all blackmail. That fetish of respectability — of what the neighbours would say . . . Murder had been committed time and again to save the murderer's respectability. And yet, he thought, so few people, if every incident in their lives became suddenly known, were respectable.

'Was that the only reason you kept this to yourself?' he asked.

'Isn't it reason enough?' she said, in that colourless tone that blent with the expression in the dull eyes. 'Do you think I wanted everyone in the village to know that I was married to a criminal — a man who had been in gaol . . . '

Mr. Budd nodded sympathetically.

'I can understand what you mean,' he said, 'but when it comes to murder . . . '

'I know nothing about that,' she broke in quickly with a tinge of life coming back into her voice. 'I know nothing that could help the police in that . . . '

'You should have let us be the best judge of that, m'am,' said the stout superintendent shaking his head. 'We don't want to make trouble for people, you know. Unless it was necessary to the clearing up of these crimes, there would've been no reason why your relationship with the dead man should have become public property. If only people 'ud realise that the police are always willin' to respect a confidence, it 'ud be much easier for everybody concerned. It's this stupid hidin' up that makes so much trouble an' work. An' it don't do any good in the long run. We always find out, you know.'

Miss Titmarsh said nothing.

'Now,' went on Mr. Budd, 'when did you last see your husband?'

After a moments hesitation she told him. She told him exactly what she had told Harry Bates, and that nervous man, listening in the kitchen, heard every word.

Would she mention anything about him, he thought uneasily. She might. There was no reason why she shouldn't, now that the police had discovered for themselves the truth about her . . .

Harry had no wish to be discovered there by Mr. Budd. The high hopes with which he had set out on this journey had come to nought. He wasn't sure whether the woman knew more than she had said or not, but if she did, it was pretty certain that she wasn't going to divulge it. The best thing he could do would be to make himself scarce while the going was good.

The back door was just behind him and he moved stealthily over to it. It was locked and bolted — Miss Titmarsh, or Mrs. Sprigot, whichever you liked to call her — was evidently a nervous woman. Well, maybe she had cause. It depended how much she really knew about the whole business. Harry softly turned the key in the lock and then set about easing back the bolts. They fitted tightly and he dare not risk making a noise. It took him a little while but he succeeded at last, and opened the door.

There was a little, narrow path that joined the main path to the front gate, and softly closing the door behind him, Harry tip-toed down the path to the gate.

His hand was on the latch when a shadow loomed up in front of him — a thin, lanky shadow that seemed to have been lurking in the gloom of the wall.

'Hello,' said a lugubrious voice. 'Who

are you an' what are yer doin' sneakin' out like that?'

Harry Bates had heard that voice before. It belonged to Sergeant Leek.

* * *

'Well, well,' remarked Mr. Budd, a few minutes later, eyeing Harry Bates and Leek as they faced him in Miss Titmarsh's little sitting room. 'So you're 'ere, are you, Harry? Two minds with but a single thought, eh?'

'Any reason why I shouldn't visit the widow of me old friend?' asked Harry in an injured voice. 'It's a nice thing if a chap can't pay a visit without gettin' collared by the police.'

'I wouldn't call it 'collared', Harry,' remonstrated the big man gently. 'I'd call it just takin' an interest in you. So you've been payin' a visit to your old friend's widow, eh? Hoping she might be able to tell you somethin' about that old friend, I s'pose?'

'Perhaps,' retorted Harry. 'Is that any concern of yours?'

'It's the concern of every member of the police force at the moment,' said Mr. Budd extravagantly. 'This is a murder job, you know, Harry, an' I wouldn't like to think that you was mixed up in it.'

A flicker of alarm came and went in Mr. Bates's eyes.

'You can't connect me with it,' he said sharply. 'I 'ad nothing' to do with it and you know it . . . '

Mr. Budd shook his head sorrowfully.

'I don't know it,' he said. 'I don't know who's mixed up in it. That's what I'm here for — to find out.' He turned to the frightened Miss Titmarsh. 'Now, m'am,' he continued, 'we was getting along nicely when we was interrupted. It was about Sam Sprigot's last visit to you that we were talking about . . . '

'I've told you all I know,' whispered Miss Titmarsh.

'Maybe you've told me all you *think* you know,' corrected the stout superintendent. 'You'd be surprised how many people think they've told all they know until somebody starts questioning 'em, an' then they remember all kinds of odd things that they'd forgot. Why did Sam come to see you?'

'I've told you,' she answered. 'He wanted me to put him up for a week or two. Of course, I refused . . . '

'And he said,' pursued Mr. Budd, 'that he was going to make the people at Marbury Court pay?'

'Yes,' she replied.

'Now, think very carefully,' said the big man. 'Did he say anything else in connection with that — anything at all?'

Miss Titmarsh started to shake her head and then stopped.

'He did say something else,' she said, frowning. 'He was laughing when he said it as though it was a joke . . . '

'What did he say?' asked the stout superintendent.

'He said . . . ' she puckered up her forehead in an effort of recollection. 'He said something about it was always good to know where the body was buried . . . '

'You never told me that,' snapped Harry Bates.

'I'd forgotten it,' she answered.

'H'm,' remarked Mr. Budd raising his

eyebrows and scratching the lowest of his many chins. 'It's always good to know where the body's buried, eh? H'm. Well, now, I wonder just what he meant by that?'

'It's a well-known expression,' said Leek. 'Meanin' that you know somethin' about somebody that they wouldn't want anyone ter know.'

Mr. Budd gave him a withering look.

'It's a wonder to me,' he said, 'how you manage to think these things out. It surprises me that you don't suffer from a perpetual headache.'

'I've got a lot of general knowledge that comes in useful,' said the lean sergeant complacently. 'It's remarkable what a lot o' things I know.'

'It's even more remarkable what a lot of things you don't,' snarled Mr. Budd. He turned back to Miss Titmarsh. 'This visit from your husband was several months ago, wasn't it?'

'Yes.' Miss Titmarsh nodded.

'He couldn't have been out of prison very long when he came to see you,' murmured Mr. Budd thoughtfully.

'He wasn't,' said Miss Titmarsh. 'Oh, you can't imagine the disgrace of it all — being married to a man like that . . . '

Her troubled face twisted and she gripped the back of the chair until her thin knuckles were milk-white.

'Very nasty for you, m'am,' said the stout superintendent sympathetically. 'What happened to 'im after he left you? When you wouldn't let him stay?'

'He went to Greystock and took lodgings there,' said Miss Titmarsh. 'I had to give him all my savings — a little over a hundred pounds. I took the money over to him as soon as I could get it out of the post office. He — he threatened to make our relationship public unless I — I helped him . . . '

A nasty bit of work, Sam, thought Mr. Budd, but it wasn't getting him any nearer finding out who had killed him. Was it at Greystock that he spent that unaccountable three months?

'How long was he at Greystock?' he asked.

'I don't know exactly,' she replied. 'I hoped he had gone. I prayed that he would go and that I could feel safe again — safe from any scandal . . . '

Mr. Budd could imagine how it had worried her. No wonder she looked scared. She had been terrified that something would come out to destroy the respectability she had built up . . .

'Look here,' broke in Harry Bates. 'I don't want to hang about here all the blessed night. You've got nothing on me, any of you. I want to get back to London . . . '

'That's all right, Harry,' said Mr. Budd genially. 'You can go anywhere you like. I'm not stoppin' you. But, if you take my advice you'll be careful. Keep out of this business, Harry. It's nasty an' dangerous. I wouldn't like to find you like they found Sam . . . '

Mr. Bates's face lost some of its colour.

'What d'you mean?' he muttered. 'You don't think . . . '

'If you don't know anythin',' advised the big man, 'don't *try* to know anythin' . . . '

'I don't know anything,' said Harry quickly.

'I don't think you do. I think you was only hopin' to,' said Mr. Budd. 'There's nothin' in this business for you, Harry . . . '

Harry Bates grinned suddenly.

'We have to make a living somehow,' he said shrugging his shoulders. 'I thought there might be pickings.' He looked quickly from one to the other of them. 'I think I'll be off,' he said. 'Maybe I can just get a train back . . . '

'Leek 'ull take you to the station,' said Mr. Budd, 'an' see you safely on your way.'

'There's no need to . . . ' began Harry.

'I'd like to make sure you get there,' interrupted the stout superintendent. 'It's a lonely walk to the station . . . '

Sergeant Leek looked as though he would have preferred to remain where he was. Quite obviously he didn't relish the assignment of seeing Harry Bates safely in the train for London, but an order was an order and he had to make the best of it.

'Now, m'am,' said Mr. Budd, when they had gone, 'there's no need for you to worry yourself any more. If the only connection that you've got with this affair is the fact that you was Sam Sprigot's wife, you needn't have any fear that it'll be made public property.'

The thin face of Miss Titmarsh lost something of its scared expression.

'I've been so frightened,' she said, 'so very frightened that it would all come out . . .'

'You've lived here quite a long time, haven't you?' asked Mr. Budd.

'Oh, yes,' she answered. 'Many, many years . . .'

'Then you may be able to help me,' said the stout superintendent and proceeded to tell her how.

16

During the next two days Mr. Budd was very busy indeed.

On the morning following his talk with Miss Titmarsh, he went over to Greystock and had a conference with Superintendent Sones, the result of which was to make that worthy official look more astonished than ever he had done in his life before. From Greystock, the stout superintendent took a train to London and spent some hours at Scotland Yard. From here he sought out the firm of estate agents who had let the flat from which the redoubtable Mr. Sprigot had descended into the waiting arms of the law.

The manager of the estate agents listened to what Mr. Budd had to say and did his best to supply the information that the big man wanted.

'Mr. Danesford gave up the flat soon after the robbery,' he said. 'I'm afraid I can't tell you where he is at present. It was quite a long time ago, you know.'

'I realise that,' said Mr. Budd. 'Did you ever meet him personally?'

'Oh, yes,' answered the manager. 'Twice, as a matter of fact. When he first came to us to find him a flat and again when he signed the agreement.'

Mr. Budd produced from an inside pocket of his overcoat a photograph.

'Do you recognize that?' he asked.

The manager looked at it.

'Yes,' he said. 'This is a photograph of Mr. Danesford.'

'I thought maybe it was,' remarked the stout superintendent, and there was nothing to show in his expression the sudden elation which filled him. His theory was receiving confirmation. At last he began to feel that he was on the right track.

'I hope,' said the manager, 'there's nothing wrong?'

'No, there's somethin' right,' said Mr. Budd.

'Mr. Danesford's a very nice gentleman,' began the manager.

'*Was*,' corrected Mr. Budd gently.

'Do you mean he's dead?' asked the astonished manager.

'I'm afraid he is,' said Mr. Budd with a sigh, as he replaced the photograph in his pocket. 'I'm very much afraid he is.'

Later that afternoon, the big man sought an interview with Colonel Blair.

The dapper assistant commissioner of the C.I.D. listened to what he had to say with growing amazement. When Mr. Budd had finished, he passed a well-manicured hand over his neat grey head.

'Have you any real proof for all this?' he asked.

Mr. Budd shook his head slowly.

'No, sir,' he answered. 'Not the kind o' proof that 'ud be any use in a Court. But I'm sure I'm right.'

'Probably you are,' said Colonel Blair, 'but you'll have to have indisputable evidence before we can act. There are still a lot of loose ends . . . '

'I know that, sir,' agreed the big man, 'but I think I can tie 'em up pretty soon.'

The assistant commissioner, who had known Mr. Budd tie up a great number of loose ends during the course of his career, thought so too. He said:

'How do you propose to set about it?'

Mr. Budd raised his heavy-lidded eyes and looked sleepily at his questioner.

'I want to find a surgeon who performed a certain operation, sir,' he answered cryptically.

Colonel Blair smiled. He was fully aware of the stout man's love of mystification. It was a boyish attribute that few would have suspected, and it was coupled with a predilection for the dramatic.

'All right,' he said, raising his eyebrows. 'I'll buy it.'

'It was an operation on a knee-cap,' said Mr. Budd. 'A smashed knee-cap. It was mended with silver wire . . . '

'I don't know what you're talking about,' said the assistant commissioner, shaking his head, 'but I am quite sure you do . . . '

'Well, you'd be right in a way, sir,' admitted the big man. 'The knee-cap was broken by a cricket ball, but you see, this silver wire wouldn't fade away. It'd be visible in an X-ray photograph for instance . . . '

'I think I'm beginning to understand what you mean,' said Colonel Blair shrewdly.

'I rather thought you might, sir,' said Mr. Budd.

'How did you find out about this — this broken kneecap?' asked the assistant commissioner curiously.

'Information received,' answered Mr. Budd with a twinkle in his eye. 'I was hopin' to find something of the sort — not a knee-cap, p'raps, but something . . . '

'The knee-cap was a bit of luck,' said Colonel Blair.

'It was better than I expected,' answered the big man.

'It's the sort of evidence a jury likes,' said Colonel Blair.

'It's the sort of evidence *I* like,' said Mr. Budd. 'It's certain an' conclusive.'

Colonel Blair picked up a pencil and thoughtfully rolled it up and down his blotting pad. His neat brows were drawn together.

'It still leaves you with a lot to do, though,' he said.

The stout superintendent got heavily to his feet.

'I know that,' he said wearily, 'nobody knows that better than what I do . . . '

* * *

'I remember the case very well,' said the surgeon. 'It was rather an unusual case, as a matter of fact. I suppose that's why I recall it so easily. Very successful too.'

'There'd be no trace of a limp, sir?' asked Mr. Budd.

'Only at first,' replied the surgeon. 'It would soon wear off. Nasty fracture, though, it was. Cricket ball caught him smack on the knee. Must have been a terrific crack, eh? Straight off the bat . . . '

'Yes, sir,' said Mr. Budd.

The grey-haired, elderly surgeon looked at him curiously.

'What is this all in aid of?' he asked. 'Why are you so interested in this operation? It was a very long time ago . . . '

'I'd rather not explain just at present,' said the big man.

'I suppose it's got to do with this murder business at Marbury? said the surgeon. 'Shocking affair. I read about it in the papers . . . '

'Maybe you'll read a lot more about it soon,' said Mr. Budd non-commitally and took his departure.

★ ★ ★

'This what you want?' said the radiologist holding up a still wet plate.

Mr. Budd peered at the large, cloudy picture with its darker markings.

'I suppose it is,' he said. 'Those dark bits are the silver wires, eh?'

The radiologist nodded.

'That's right,' he said. 'Old compound fracture of the knee-cap by the look of it.'

'Can I have three or four copies of it?' asked the big superintendent.

'Yes.'

'How soon can I have 'em?'

The radiologist considered.

'Have 'em ready for you this evening

— say about five-thirty,' he replied.

'I'll come and collect them at six,' said Mr. Budd.

★   ★   ★

Sergeant Leek was a little disgruntled.

For nearly three days he had seen very little of his superior. With an attack of unusual energy, Mr. Budd was in and out of Kenwiddy's farm, only staying for a few minutes sometimes and once not returning until the following day. During the short periods when he *was* there, Leek tried to get him to talk, but the stout superintendent refused to discuss anything. He seemed in a remarkably good temper which the melancholy sergeant, from long experience, took to be a sign that things were going well, but he was as close as the proverbial oyster.

Leek, in consequence, was not only annoyed but curious. Even the notes for his book of reminiscences failed to interest him.

What was Mr. Budd up to?

Somehow or other, he had found a line

to the solution of the case, but what was it?

Leek strongly objected to being left out in the cold. It was always the way, he thought, gloomily. If there was any unpleasant work to be done, it always fell to him. But when things were plain-sailing, Budd preferred to deal with them himself. He liked to spring surprises, even on his own associates. Liked to be dramatic, that was his trouble.

But it was useless trying to get him to say anything before he was ready. Trying to prise open a steel safe with a meat skewer would be easier than getting information out of Mr. Budd until he was prepared to divulge it.

It was the evening of the fourth day when the stout superintendent came back to the farm after being absent on one of his mysterious trips and sought out Leek in the big sitting room.

'Get your coat on,' he said abruptly, 'we're goin' out.'

'Where?' asked Leek.

'Up to Marbury Court,' replied the big man shortly.

'What are we goin' up there for?' inquired the sergeant curiously.

'You'll see, when we get there,' retorted Mr. Budd.

Leek sighed. He was still to be kept in the dark, apparently. He pulled on his coat and they set off. Mr. Budd was silent during the walk, but Leek judged by his expression that he was very pleased with himself.

Lupton admitted them, and Mr. Budd asked to see Mr. Titer. They were shown into a small room opening off the hall, and the butler went in search of the solicitor.

After a short while, Mr. Titer came in.

'You wished to see me?' he inquired unnecessarily. 'You have — er — news?'

'I think so, sir,' said Mr. Budd. 'I believe I have news of Mr. Francis Conyers.'

Mr. Titer's usually expressionless face for once expressed surprise.

'Indeed,' he said. 'Do you mean that you have — er — found him?'

'Yes, I've found him,' said Mr. Budd.

'Is he alive?' asked the lawyer.

'No, sir,' answered Mr. Budd shaking his head. 'No, I'm afraid he's not alive . . . '

'Dear me,' said Mr. Titer frowning. 'I don't quite understand — er — Superintendent. When did he die — where . . . ?'

'He died,' said Mr. Budd slowly and carefully, 'a few nights ago . . . '

'A few nights ago,' echoed the now thoroughly astonished lawyer.

'As to how and where he died,' continued Mr. Budd, 'he died from a heavy blow on the head in the hall of that old, ruined house, Jackson's Folly.'

'But that's nonsense,' ejaculated Mr. Titer. 'That was Sir Basil . . . '

'No, sir,' answered Mr. Budd. 'That was Francis, his younger brother. The man you have always believed to be Sir Basil Conyers has always been Francis, sir, from the time he took his brother's identity to inherit the estate.'

17

The rather prominent adam's apple in Mr. Titer's stringy throat moved convulsively up and down as he appeared to have difficulty in swallowing. Leek's face was the picture of incredulous astonishment.

If Mr. Budd had intended to spring a surprise he had succeeded.

'But — but,' stammered the lawyer, 'this — this is incredible. It's absurd! There must be a mistake . . .

'There's no mistake,' said Mr. Budd. 'The man who was killed in Jackson's Folly was Francis Conyers . . . '

'I can't believe it,' declared Mr. Titer. 'I can't believe it. Do you mean that — that Sir Basil has never *been* Sir Basil . . . ?'

'Yes,' said Mr. Budd, 'that's exactly what I do mean.'

'But . . . Of course you can produce proof of this astounding assertion?' said Mr. Titer. It was obvious that he had received the greatest shock of his somewhat uneventful life.

'I can produce all the proof that's necessary,' answered the stout superintendent. 'I don't know whether you are aware of it, you may be and you may be not — it doesn't really matter — but when Francis Conyers was at Oxford he suffered an accident to his left knee. A cricket ball hit him an' fractured the knee-cap . . . '

'Yes, yes, I remember,' said Mr. Titer.

'There was an operation,' continued Mr. Budd, 'an' the knee-cap had to be fastened with silver wire. It didn't affect his walking when once he'd recovered, but the silver wire remained. I've seen the surgeon who performed the operation an' I've got his testimony, signed an' witnessed.'

'I still don't quite understand,' began Mr. Titer frowning.

'Those silver wires 'ud show in an X-ray photograph to this day,' continued Mr. Budd. 'In fact they *do* show.'

He unwrapped a parcel which he had been carrying under his arm, took out a large photographic film and held it up to the light.

'This is an X-ray photograph of the left knee of the man who was killed — the man everyone believed was Sir Basil Conyers. If you look, you'll see the dark marks in the knee-cap where the fracture was originally fastened with the silver wire.'

Mr. Titer peered at the photograph.

'I can see certain marks,' he admitted cautiously, 'but . . . '

'The radiologist who took this photograph will testify that those marks are the silver wires, sir,' said Mr. Budd. 'I think that'll be sufficient proof that the body is that of Francis an' not Sir Basil Conyers.'

Mr. Titer fingered his chin.

'It seems to be fairly conclusive,' he said reluctantly. 'But . . . really the whole thing is incredible — incredible. Surely we should have noticed the difference between Sir Basil and his brother?'

'I don't think you would — I don't think anyone would,' said Mr. Budd. 'They were very much alike an' nobody had seen Francis for several years. The greatest difference was that Francis was clean shaven an' Basil had a moustache . . . '

'But . . . Good gracious!' exclaimed the lawyer as a sudden startling thought struck him. 'If, as you affirm, the man who has been living here all this time was Francis, what happened to Basil?'

'Accordin' to my theory,' said Mr. Budd quietly, 'Basil is dead . . . '

'I concluded something of the sort,' said Mr. Titer dryly. 'I can hardly imagine that he would have let his brother annex the estate if he had been alive. Is it your suggestion that — he was killed?'

The stout superintendent nodded.

'I believe he was murdered — by Francis,' he said.

Mr. Titer, in receipt of this further shock, obviously felt unable to deal with it standing up. Pulling out a chair, he sat down, motioning to Mr. Budd to do the same.

The big man did so and was promptly followed by Leek, who never remained standing if he could help it.

'Now,' said the lawyer, taking out his

handkerchief and wiping his face carefully, 'I should be obliged if you would be a trifle clearer. What are you suggesting happened exactly?'

Mr. Budd coughed.

'Well, sir,' he said, 'what I believe happened was this. For some time before Sir Thomas Conyers died, Basil Conyers was abroad — in Switzerland, I think. It's my opinion that while he was there he met his brother Francis who had fled abroad, earlier, after the trouble over the forged cheque. I believe they were both in Switzerland when the news of Sir Thomas's death reached them. I think that Francis travelled back with Basil when Basil came to claim his inheritance. Probably Basil, who from what I can discover from people who knew him in the past, was a good-natured sort of chap, suggested that he should. Likely enough he offered to help him now that his father was dead. The suggestion may have come from Francis, we'll never be able to say definitely, but I'm convinced that he had already got the idea in his mind of doing away with his brother an' taking his place.'

'This is all conjecture, isn't it?' interrupted Mr. Titer.

'Up to a point it is,' admitted Mr. Budd, 'but there're certain bits of evidence to back it up, an' I think there'll be a final, conclusive, bit later. You see, what put me on to this, when I was searching for a theory that 'ud fit the facts, was the behaviour of Sir Basil.'

'The behaviour of Sir Basil?' questioned Mr. Titer frowning.

'All this gambling and women chasin',' replied Mr. Budd. 'It wasn't in character — not from what I gathered from his early life. But it *was* in the character of his brother, Francis. He'd always been a gambler an' a scoundrel. Why had Sir Basil suddenly changed after he'd come into the property?'

'Yes, I see what you mean,' said Mr. Titer nodding. 'That was rather shrewd of you Superintendent. We all thought it rather surprising but we never imagined the real reason.'

'Francis Conyers took his brother's place, married, an' settled down at

231

Marbury Court,' continued Mr. Budd. 'But he had a flat in London in the name of Danesford . . . '

'A flat in London,' echoed Mr. Titer.

The big man nodded.

'That's a proved fact,' he said. 'The manager of the estate agents who let it to 'im recognized his photograph. I should say he took the flat in another name so that he could carry on as he liked without his wife knowing. He didn't want any trouble with her because of her money. But trouble was comin' to him quick enough. Sam Sprigot made a mistake an' broke into the wrong flat one night. It was Danesford's. Danesford wasn't there — he was down at Marbury Court in his own character of Sir Basil — but there was certain things there which interested Sam very mightily. There was snapshots of Francis Conyers — a lot of 'em — snaps which had been taken at Marbury Court as Sir Basil an' Sam recognized an old friend. He'd known Francis in the old days before the forged cheque business had driven him abroad an' he thought, now that he was back in England, he'd look him up. Unfortunately for Sam he was pinched as he left the flat an' sent to prison for a stretch. But he'd made up his mind what he was goin' to do when he came out of stir, an' he did it. He came down to Greystock — ' Mr. Budd carefully refrained from mentioning Miss Titmarsh ' — an' he managed to get hold of Sir Basil somehow. Prob'ly met him when he was out. Sam greeted him as an old friend, an' although Sir Basil tried to bluff that he *was* Sir Basil an' not Francis, Sam wasn't fooled. He wanted a cut in his former friend's good fortune an' he meant to have it. Francis was at his wits end. He had very little money of his own fortune left — not enough to satisfy Sam's demands — an' to add to his troubles his wife, somehow or other, had begun to suspect the truth — that he was really Francis.

'He was in a pretty dangerous mess, an' he knew it. He managed to stall Sam off by promising to pay him what he wanted if he'd wait for a few months. Sam was a bit reluctant but he eventually agreed. One of the conditions Francis made was that he should clear out of Greystock, which he did an' took a room with Mrs. Bagley off the Waterloo Road. But he didn't trust Francis. He knew that Francis had somehow or other done away with his brother, an' Sam was scared that he might try the same with him.

'In the meanwhile, Francis was gettin' in a panic. He'd tried to borrow money from his wife but she'd refused, an' he didn't know which way to turn. There was, as far as he could see, only one way out — Lady Conyers would have to die. But, unless he was very careful, he'd be bound to be suspected. Sam Sprigot for one, would definitely guess who was responsible for her death and that would give him a greater hold than before.

'There was only one really safe way. Sam would have to die too, an' his death must be made to link with the death of Lady Conyers. Francis laid his plans an', when he was ready, he wrote Sam makin' an appointment in Jackson's Folly. On the same night he put cyanide in the glass of water which he knew Lady Conyers always used to take her sleeping tablet.

'Sam was scared of Francis but he was greedy and he came. What happened to him you know. Francis killed him, scrawled that bit out of the nursery rhyme on the front door of Jackson's Folly so that, when the other bit o' the same rhyme was found on the door of the room in which Lady Conyers was lying dead, there'd appear to be a connection between the two deaths. To link his dead wife still more with Sam's murder, Francis left her scarf on the post of the staircase in Jackson's Folly.'

Mr. Titer gently stroked his chin. He had received a shock and, although his habitual calmness had not quite deserted him, it had been considerably shaken.

'You — er — appear to have worked it out very well, Superintendent,' he said after a pause. 'But, as I said before, the greater part of what you say is pure conjecture . . .'

'It can't be anythin' else,' agreed Mr. Budd, 'but it fits the facts we have got, an' every fresh fact that I've managed to get hold of confirms it.'

'There is one thing,' said the lawyer

frowning, 'that rather upsets your theory — I don't say it destroys it but it requires an explanation . . . '

'I know what your goin' to say, sir,' broke in Mr. Budd. 'You're goin' to say, if all this other part is true, who killed Francis?'

'Exactly,' said Mr. Titer.

'I'll be comin' to that later,' said the big man. 'It seems to me that there's only one person who could've done that. But I'd rather not go into it at present . . . '

Mr. Titer gave him a shrewd glance.

'I can anticipate the trend of your thoughts,' he said. 'I hope that I may be wrong . . . ' He shook his head. 'With regard to your — er — theory regarding the — er — exchange of identity between Basil and Francis. Where do you imagine this took place?'

'Do you mean where did Francis murder his brother?' said Mr. Budd, and the lawyer nodded. 'Well,' continued the big man slowly, 'It's my opinion, an' we'll be able to put it to the test pretty soon, that Francis killed his brother not so very far from here . . . '

Mr. Titer looked at him sharply.

'You mean . . ?' he began and stopped abruptly.

'I mean,' finished Mr. Budd, 'that it's my belief that he killed him in Jackson's Folly an' we'll find the body buried somewhere in the ruins of that old house.'

★   ★   ★

There was a great deal of activity amid the dust and decay of Jackson's Folly. A small army of men with picks and shovels, spades and crowbars, invaded the old ruin and set to work to prove Mr. Budd's theory.

The news that something was afoot ran round the village like a streak of wild-fire and they had a job to keep the curious sightseers at a distance.

Mr. Budd, himself, conducted operations, accompanied by the lugubrious Sergeant Leek, and if he felt any anxiety as to the result of the operations he had started, it didn't show on his bovine, stolid face.

To a certain extent his reputation was

at stake. He had, unlike anything he had done before, built up his theory on pure conjecture, founded on a few definite facts. He had imagined what might have happened from the meagre information at his disposal and was now trying to prove that he was correct.

So far he had been proved right. His idea that Francis had taken his brother's place and passed himself off as Basil Conyers had been right. When the idea had first struck him he had racked his brain to find some method of proving it. Was there anything that would show the difference between the two brothers? Anything that could have survived the years? And he had been lucky when inquiries had brought to light the fractured knee-cap. There was no argument about *that*. It was something that even the most sceptical of juries would have to believe.

Would the rest of this theory receive the same proof?

It was, he admitted to himself, a long shot in the dark to conclude that Francis had killed his brother in Jackson's Folly and hidden the body there, but it was founded on a little more than just a probability.

The murder had to take place somewhere where it was possible to dispose of the body so that it was unlikely to be found. There was, of course, the possibility that Francis had killed Basil abroad, but the difficulty of concealing the body would have been much greater than if he had waited until they reached England. Francis must, in his younger days, have often seen the old house, falling to ruins, when he had been at Marbury Court. What more logical conclusion than to suppose that when the idea of doing away with his brother and taking his place had first come to Francis, and he was seeking for a means of concealing his crime, that the old house should have occurred to him?

It would have been easy to find some excuse for getting Basil, on their way to Marbury Court, to go to Jackson's Folly. Francis was clever enough to have arranged it that their arrival should be after dark and it was a hundred chances to one that anyone would see them. Having disposed of Basil and hidden the body, he could have gone back to London, waited a few days — he must have already allowed his moustache to grow — and then turned up at Marbury Court as though he had just arrived from abroad.

Nobody was likely to question his identity. He was sufficiently like Basil to pass with most people, and nobody was likely to make inquiries as to the exact date and means by which he had arrived in England.

It was a shot in the dark, thought Mr. Budd as he watched his men searching among the debris and rubble but it was based on sound reasoning.

It was a long job. For nearly two days they worked diligently without any result for their labours, and Mr. Budd was beginning to feel that his reasoning had not been so sound as he had imagined.

And then, on the afternoon of the third day, they found what they had been searching for.

It lay in a shallow grave beneath the

floorboards of the wrecked drawing room — an unrecognizable thing in rags of clothing that had nearly rotted away from time and damp. But there was no doubt how death had come. The back of the skull was crushed in. Basil had died in the same way as Sam Sprigot had died — in the same way that his murderer had died — from a heavy blow on the back of the head.

Mr. Budd stared stolidly down at the body

His reasoning had been justified.

18

The village of Marbury seethed with excitement. The news of the gruesome discovery was the final touch to the excitement of the last few weeks.

The Reverend Oswald Hornbeam met Major Panting in the High Street soon after the discovery had been made and was instantly button-holed by that excited individual.

'I suppose you've heard?' said the major. 'By jove, what do you think of it, eh?'

The rector shook his head.

'It's terrible — terrible,' he answered. 'I told you that evil had been loosed in the village . . . '

'They tell me that the body was Basil Conyers,' said Major Panting. 'The feller we all thought was Sir Basil was his brother, Francis . . . '

'Cain and Abel,' said the Reverend Oswald. 'Really shocking . . . '

'Always was a scoundrel,' said the major. 'Remember him as a young man . . .'

'He suffered his deserts,' said the rector soberly. 'Poor fellow . . .'

'Deserved all he got in my opinion,' declared Major Panting. 'What I can't understand, is who killed *him*. That's still a bit of a puzzle, eh?'

'No doubt that will come out in time,' said the rector. 'It saddens me to think that there should be so much wickedness in my parish. I feel that in some way I have failed . . .'

'Rubbish,' broke in the major. 'Not your fault. People are as they're made. Pretty nasty most of 'em . . .'

The Reverend Oswald shook his head sorrowfully.

'I should not like to believe that,' he said. 'I always try to seek the good in even the worst of us . . .'

'But you don't often find it, I'll be bound,' said Major Panting. 'Precious little good in Francis Conyers. Killed his brother, killed his wife, and I suppose killed the crook feller too. Three murders, eh? Have to seek a long time to find any good in him.'

The Reverend Oswald Hornbeam sighed. 'Human nature is a strange mixture,' he said. 'There must have been some good in him somewhere. Nobody is all evil . . . '

He went on his way, still shaking his head, and Major Panting walked on up the High Street, looking sharply out for somebody else with whom he could discuss the astounding news.

Mr. Budd, after the discovery, had disappeared.

He left Marbury later on the same afternoon and didn't return until the following morning, when he went up to his room at Kenwiddy's Farm and was not seen again until later that night. But Sergeant Leek was unusually active. He and Inspector Crutchley spent a long time together and were joined by Superintendent Sones.

All three of them looked very grave. As well they might for the end was approaching and they were all three facing a difficult ordeal.

★   ★   ★

It was a dark night with a high wind and a drizzle of rain, when Harry Bates got out of the train at Marbury, gave up his ticket to the porter on duty, and made his way down the slope to the road.

The wind was cold and he huddled into his heavy overcoat as he walked quickly along. He was not, to judge by the expression on his face, feeling very happy at whatever prospect lay before him.

Along the open country road he trudged along, once pausing to light a cigarette and glance at his watch. It was a quarter to ten. He had nearly an hour before his appointment.

Coming to the cross-roads, he turned into the right hand road, out of which, further along, led the narrow lane which ended at the patch of open country before the gate of Jackson's Folly. But Harry Bates ignored the mouth of the lane and kept on until he came to the grounds of Marbury Court. At a gate set in a high hedge, he stopped. He could see from here the lights of the village shining dimly and particularly the lights of the Bull.

He passed his tongue over his dry lips.

He would have given a lot for a drink but he daren't risk it. He had no wish to be seen.

The rain was increasing and the wind whistled round him, seeking every means to penetrate the protection of his overcoat and probe with icy fingers his already shivering body.

A clock struck the hour.

Harry Bates counted the ten strokes and thought with dismay that he had another three-quarters of an hour to wait.

His feet were getting numb with the cold and damp and he tried to warm them, but it did little good. However, the result of this night's work might prove to be profitable. He didn't relish the job, but it would soon be over.

The clock struck the quarter.

Half an hour more. He began to walk up and down in front of the gate. It was too early yet to make his way inside the grounds of Marbury Court to the little summer house. He might be seen.

At half past ten he decided to risk it. It would be something to get in the shelter, away from the rain and the wind.

He pushed open the gate and slipped inside. It was very dark here, and he wasn't quite sure of his way. There was a path that led through a shrubbery of rhododendron bushes and came out at the end of a lawn. From here he could see, a good way away, the dim bulk of the house. There were lights in one or two of the windows but the majority were dark . . .

Ah, there was the summer house — over to the right of the oblong lawn. Harry changed his direction and made his way towards it. It was only a small place of rustic wood with a couple of garden chairs and a wooden table, but it was shelter from the increasing rain and the wind.

Harry went inside and breathed a little sigh of relief. He thought of hot coffee and the warmth of 'Spotties' or the tingle of neat whisky. Well, he'd be able to enjoy either or both of these comforts when this night's work was over.

There was no sound but the wind in the trees and the pattering of the falling rain on the leaves and on the roof.

Somewhere, far away in the distance, he heard the faint sound of a train whistle, but that was all. Otherwise there was complete silence.

And then the clock struck the three-quarters.

A quarter to eleven. It was time.

Harry felt his nerves tighten to meet the ordeal he was facing. In a few seconds now the person he was here to meet would arrive. Tense in the darkness of the summer house, he waited.

There was nothing to warn him of anyone's approach. The first he knew that he was no longer alone was when he heard the sound of quick breathing from the direction of the door.

'Are you there?' inquired a voice from the darkness.

'Yes,' said Harry Bates.

'I came,' went on the voice, 'though I quite fail to understand the meaning of your letter.'

'It was plain enough,' said Harry.

'What it *said* was plain enough,' corrected the newcomer. 'But I don't understand your implication . . . '

'Look here,' interrupted Harry Bates, 'it's no good you adopting that attitude. I'm not going to stop here all night arguing. If you want me to keep quiet about a certain thing, you've got to pay me — and pay me well. Otherwise I'm going to the police, see?'

'I hear what you say,' replied the voice. 'I'd like to remind you that blackmail is dangerous . . . '

'You can cut out the threats,' broke in Harry roughly. 'I'm not scared by 'em. You can't murder me like you murdered Francis Conyers.'

Out of the darkness came a sudden hissing breath.

'You can't prove that,' said the voice sharply.

'Can't I?' retorted Harry, 'You refuse to do what I tell you and you'll soon see whether I can prove it or not.'

There was a moments silence but he still heard the other breathing.

'What is it you want?' came the question at last.

'I want five thousand pounds,' answered Harry Bates promptly.

'I haven't anything near such a sum,' said the voice.

'But you will have,' snapped Harry. 'I'll wait.'

'Supposing I refuse?'

'I've told you the alternative,' said Harry.

'There is another,' said the voice and now it held a sharper note. Something, a sixth sense or a movement that reached him in time, warned Harry Bates. Springing sideways he caught an arm as it was descending and the knife it held cut his wrist. He felt the warm blood trickling over his hand as he fought off his attacker.

And then there was a shout and a sudden blaze of light. The ray of a powerful electric torch lit up the inside of the summer house as Mr. Budd, Sergeant Leek and Inspector Crutchley burst out from the concealment of the nearby bushes.

'Grab 'er,' shouted Mr. Budd, and Crutchley leapt forward and caught Mrs. Mortlock's arm just as she had wrested free from Harry's grip and was raising her arm to bring down the knife . . .

★ ★ ★

Harry Bates gulped down the greater portion of a double scotch, and took a deep breath.

'Cor blind old Riley!' he ejaculated with intense feeling, 'I wouldn't go through that again for all the gold in the Bank of England.'

'I'll bet you would, Harry,' said Mr. Budd. 'Not that anyone's likely to try you.'

'Honestly,' said Harry Bates, 'my heart was playing such acrobatic tricks I thought it was going to jump clean out of me mouth. What a Tarter, eh?'

'You did very well, Harry,' said the stout superintendent. 'Maybe one day, I'll be able to do you a good turn. It was the only way to get at her, you see.'

Harry swallowed the remainder of his whisky and looked meaningly at the bottle on the table. Mr. Budd reached forward and refilled his glass.

They were sitting in the warm sitting-room at Kenwiddy's Farm. Mrs. Mortlock had been taken to Greystock police station and charged with the murder of her step-brother, Francis Conyers, and the attempted murder of Harry Bates. She had protested all the way but nobody had taken any notice of her. During their ambush in the bushes near the summer house, they had both seen and heard enough to convince them of her guilt.

Mr. Budd had arranged it all with Harry Bates, a reluctant assistant who under the persuasive tongue of the stout superintendent, and the promise of certain emoluments, had at last agreed to help. The big man had been certain that the only person who had had any motive for killing Francis was Mrs. Mortlock, but he had no proof of her guilt. The only possibility of getting proof was to arrange with Harry to pretend that he knew she had committed the murder and try to blackmail her. Harry had written her, hinting what he knew and arranging the appointment in the summer house. Mr. Budd had been afraid that she might bluff. If she had and stuck to it they would have been helpless. But he had gauged her nature fairly well. She had adopted the attitude he hoped she would and her attack on Harry with murderous intentions. Coupled with the fact that she alone benefited from the death of Francis would prove sufficient to convict her.

'It's a queer thing, you know,' remarked Mr. Budd, helping himself to a small whisky and lighting one of his black, evil-smelling cigars, 'but there've been remarkably few facts to help in this business. I'd call it a case without any practical clues. It was all a question of thinkin' an' ponderin'.'

'You're a downy old bird,' said Harry. 'The boys always say there ain't much hope when you start getting busy.'

★ ★ ★

'A very nice piece of work,' said Colonel Blair, leaning back in his chair and smoothing his neat grey head with an immaculate hand. 'I should call it one of your most successful cases, Budd. You had practically nothing to go on and you've succeeded in bringing the matter to a satisfactory conclusion.'

'Thank you, sir,' said Mr. Budd.

'There was so much,' went on the assistant commissioner, 'to fog the real issue. All that business of the nursery rhyme . . .'

'An' the spy dropped by parachute,' interpolated the stout man. 'He had nothing at all to do with it.'

'He may have had quite a lot to do with Francis Conyers,' said Colonel Blair quietly, and Mr. Budd opened his sleepy eyes suddenly very wide.

'I've been talking to the man who was in charge of M.I.5 at that period,' went on Colonel Blair. 'They knew there was a 'contact' somewhere in that particular district, but they'd never been lucky enough to find out who it was. The man Panting caught, his name was Khoner, by the way, refused to tell them anything . . .'

'You think the 'contact' was Francis Conyers, sir?' asked Mr. Budd.

'I should say it was more than likely,' answered Colonel Blair. 'He was a pretty bad hat all through and I should think it was quite possible that he was in the pay of the German Secret Service. They probably got hold of him while he was in Switzerland.'

'I should say you're probably right, sir,' agreed the big man. 'In my opinion Francis Conyers was capable of anythin'.'

'I suppose Roger Marsden comes into his sister's money now?' remarked Colonel Blair.

'I think he gets the whole estate,' said Mr. Budd. 'He's the next of kin. There are no other livin' Conyers — or there won't be soon.'

'I wonder if they'll hang her?' murmured the assistant commissioner thoughtfully. 'Juries are funny with women, you know.'

'It was a particularly brutal crime, sir,' said Mr. Budd. 'An' cold-blooded. She killed him that way so'd we'd think it was the same person that killed Sam Sprigot.'

'She ought to hang,' said Colonel Blair. 'In my opinion, all murderers should hang. There's far too much fuss made over 'em these days. Nobody ever seems to think about the unfortunate victim.'

'I agree with you, sir,' said Mr. Budd,

'although in this case the victim deserved to hang as well.'

★ ★ ★

The trial of Mrs. Mortlock filled the newspapers for the two days that it lasted and then, like others like it, it was forgotten in a fresh sensation.

For some reason, perhaps it was the sheer brutality of the killing, or perhaps because of her attitude in the dock, which was callous and contemptuous, the jury took a dislike to her from the start. In spite of everything her counsel could do, they brought in a verdict of guilty after only being out for an hour and a half.

She was sentenced to death and, although a reprieve was attempted, it was refused.

Three clear Sundays after the sentence was passed on her, Mrs. Mortlock was hanged.

In Marbury the news was received without much comment. The main excitement was over and the actual carrying out of the sentence was almost an anti-climax.

'Well,' remarked Major Panting to the Reverend Oswald Hornbeam one frosty afternoon a week later, 'the whole thing's over. Settle down again to our previous dullness, eh?'

'I prefer the dullness, Panting,' said the rector. He sniffed the keen air. 'It seems to me that something has passed away leaving the whole village washed clean.'

'I know what you mean,' said Panting. 'Felt something of the sort myself.'

Mr. Budd, coming into his cheerless office one morning, found the lugubrious Sergeant Leek writing busily in his exercise book.

'Still writing your reminiscences?' he demanded.

'I'm making notes on that business at Marbury,' said the lean sergeant, looking up. 'I'm callin' it 'The Nursery Rhyme Murders'. I think that sounds excitin'.'

'It 'ud be all right for a book of fairy tales,' said Mr. Budd.

'I'm usin' it for me reminiscences,' said Leek.

'That's what I meant,' said Mr. Budd.